# Who was this man—
# and what did he want with her?

He said his name was John Collier. He claimed to have come from the heartland of the American midwest to the New England coast where the Phenwicks lived within sound of the crashing Atlantic waves.

But he refused to explain what magnet had drawn him here—or how he knew things about the Phenwicks that no other living mortal suspected.

From the moment Kate Phenwick met him, she felt his power over her—a power even greater than her handsome cousin once had used to bring her to the very brink of ruin.

This time Kate knew there would be no resisting—no matter how demonic were this man's desires, or what fearsome evil might be born from the end of her innocence and the beginning of her knowledge of what it truly meant to be a Phenwick woman. . . .

# #13
## KATHERYN KIMBROUGH'S
## Saga of the Phenwick Women

# KATE,
# THE CURIOUS

POPULAR LIBRARY • NEW YORK

# PROLOGUE

Laughable. The entire earthly concept—or at least that traditionally accepted—of that which happens afterward. Mythical. Perhaps that is a better word. I suppose I had preconceived concepts myself because of certain dogmatic teachings. There is such a natural continuity. One simply continues.

I have encountered those close to me, those with whom I had emotional bonds when I strutted and stormed among the living. Those to whom I seemed the closest then have only been as passing shadows, gray against black, as if wafting among memories. While others, toward whom I had emotional conflicts, some of which were never resolved, have been the ones with whom I have come in contact with some regularity.

For instance, many would believe that I would be in continual touch with my son Danny, because we were so close. Instead it is Margaret, whom I nearly tormented to death, that I cannot avoid. Danny and I were together for awhile—which might have been years by mortal time, but was only a few grains of sand in the overall picture of this other life.

I had thought perhaps Danny was my soul mate. That is not the case. I discovered we had been together many different lifetimes and that we had ties that would long make us kindred spirits. Ironically Danny's soul mate was in earthly attire during his lifetime, but the boy never suspected. However, they were good friends and in their last years some of that eternal love came close to expression.

The last I was aware of Danny was when he came to tell me that that other soul had reincarnated back into earthly flesh. While I understood that such was the path of the soul, I was not knowledgeable about the process. Over here when a question arises, an answer comes, I know not from where. As usual, when that information was given, I was shown the working out of the principle, permitted to observe.

I believe it was the spirit of Rosea Hackleby during one of our encounters who attempted to convince me that although an entity occupied the body of a particular sex during an incarnation he or she would *not* necessarily return to the same sex in the next lifetime. One usually spent no more than three eras in one physical type of body before it reversed back into the opposite. I presumed that I would naturally go into a male body upon my return—if that ever happened—because of the aggressive life I lived as Augusta Phenwick. Rosea said that that was not necessarily true, that I would probably choose—when the time came—to go into another degree of the feminine personality.

Another thing Rosea told me that was disturbing was that Danny had had a particular karmic tie to his daughter Rachel, and that one of the reasons she had been susceptible to invasion by alien spirits was her strong emotional tie to her father in that life, which he had not reciprocated properly. She reincarnated as his grand-daughter, the child of one of the men who had loved her during her days of torment. And those days of torment were not without reason, either. But I am not here to go into a lengthy discourse on that.

Still it is curious to see how lives intermingle and one touches again and again with kindred spirits. Observing the unfolding of such a love story takes away some of the restlessness that I have experienced. I was not shocked, simply absolutely amazed, and perhaps will grow in my own awareness.

# CHAPTER ONE

1853.

The farmhouse was isolated on the flat, level land in Illinois. The nearest settlement was a place called Fowler, probably named for the first settler who went in and set up a farm in that vast open space east of the Mississippi River. The nearest town, and that was not of any great size at the time, was a place called Quincy, which was right on the river. The railroad went through Quincy, making it a location from which farmers in the surrounding area could take their produce for shipping into the larger cities.

John Tyler Collier was the third son, the fourth child, of a family of nine children. His older brothers, Lemuel and Sam Jr., had left home several years before. Lemuel went far west, Sam Jr. rode the Mississippi, with the intention of going to Hannibal. Chances are he went as far down as St. Louis. Neither of the brothers were heard from again.

A year older than John, Abby was like a second mother to the rest of the children, taking the place that the eldest might. John never resented his sister, nor any of his siblings. At twenty-two he longed to leave home. If he had to farm, it should be on his own soil. The younger brothers were strong enough to assume their share of the duties.

Nellie Collier, just younger than John, married a farmhand. Sam Sr. gave Nellie and her man, Luke, a piece of land and helped them build a house on it. Nellie was the only one of the family in whom John would confide. Often after putting in a day's work on the Collier farm, the youth would go help Luke with his chores. Luke put in exhaustively long hours and shortly after supper, he was ready for bed and sleep.

Nellie was pregnant with her first child. It was difficult for her to sleep. She preferred sitting up, rocking on the porch during the long hot evenings of summer. She liked when John stayed for supper and sat and spoke with her, sometimes well after the stars and moon had come out.

John would rub his callused hands together and stare at them while it was still twilight. He was a good-looking boy, perhaps the best-looking of the whole Collier family. Naturally curly brown hair, sky-blue eyes, nice, soft features. While he had powerful strength from working the farm since he was a boy, he was not bulging with muscles. Shirtless, his bib overalls left no doubt that he could do a man's work.

"Sometimes ya seem so moody, John," Nellie would remark after studying his pensive expression as he gazed absently out over the level earth.

"Huh? Oh, I was just thinkin', I reckon," John replied.

"You'd think as much work as I do in a day that at night I wouldn't have time to dream. But I do."

"Dream—about what?" his sister asked. She was knitting and would continue to do so until it became too dark to see her work. "What *do* ya dream about, John?"

"The ocean."

"The ocean? Why, John Tyler Collier, you ain't never seen an ocean," she exclaimed. "The farthest east ya ever bin was Peoria. And there ain't no ocean in Peoria that I know of."

"There's the Illinois River," John said with a laugh. "It's good and wide there all right. But you're right, it's not an ocean."

"And ya've never been westa Quincy, have ya? I mean, ya never even got the other side of the Mississippi, did ya?"

"Nope, Nell, I haven't," John replied, again rubbing his hands. "But that don't keep me from dreamin' none about the ocean. I read that whole box of books Mama brought with her from Philadelphia. And I don't know how many times I've read the Bible from cover to cover."

"I remember ya used to read it to us kids when we was little," Nellie commented. "I never was much interested in readin' good. Guess that's why I never learned the big words."

"Why, I'd go crazy if I couldn't read and write," John explained. "Sometimes I write my dreams down. I dream about the same place a lot. There's always this same little cottage sorta on a cliff overlookin' the ocean. And there's a path leadin' down to the beach."

"What's a cottage?" asked Nellie.

"A cottage? Why, it's a house. That's what some people call houses."

"How do ya know?"

"I read it in a book." John rose and stretched. "Well, I reckon I better be gittin' on home to bed. I gotta get up before daybreak and take a loada grain down to Quincy. See ya later." He waved.

Nellie watched her handsome brother saunter toward the front gate. A dog named Bo followed him. "John. Ya come back here a minute." She put her knitting aside as she watched his tall silhouette return.

"What is it, Sis?"

"How much ya gonna git for that grain?"

"Maybe seven or ten dollars, if I'm lucky," he replied, scratching his head and yawning. "Why'd you ask?"

"Why don't ya take it? I've got another five dollars in the sugar bowl. Take it all and catch a riverboat and go down to Hannibal or St. Louis."

"Catch a riverboat? Why?"

"Because I got a funny feelin' about your dreams," Nellie said softly. "Now you stay here and I'll be back directly."

Before he could object, Nellie had gone into the house. He kicked the dirt with his foot, then reached down to pet Bo. His sister was back with a handful of coins.

"I counted 'em all yesterday," Nellie said, offering them to him. "It's the least we could give ya for all the work ya done around here. Maybe in Hannibal or St. Louis ya'd meet ya a nice girl. Any maybe ya can meet someone who knows what dreams are all about. Ya take your book with the dreams marked down in it with ya. I've just got a strong feelin' about this, John. Tom and Bob can take care of the farm with Dad."

John knew about Nellie's strong feelings. He accepted the money, nodded thank you and left.

"John," she called as he reached the gate, "if ya don't come back right away, write to us sometime." She patted her belly. "If it's a little boy, I'll name him John for ya."

As John walked home, about a half a mile from his sister's house, he had the impression he was going toward his own funeral. Many thoughts thundered in his brain. Confusion. Decision. He ached to know what it was like to be with a woman, to have a wife. Luke had told him it was all right and better than most other things. But Luke was never enthusiastic about anything. John wanted to know for himself.

The next morning he awakened at three, a half hour earlier than he usually did. After washing and dressing— not in his usual overalls, but a pair of trousers and a shirt—he awakened his younger brother Tom and told him to get dressed, that he was going into Quincy with him. While Tom was getting ready, he fixed breakfast for the two of them.

Wilma Collier rose, disturbed by the noise her sons were making. "Ya fixin' on goin' to Quincy so early?"

"I couldn't sleep no longer. Besides," John explained, "an early start will git us there before the heat of the day sets in."

"Ya takin' Tom with ya?" the plain-faced mother asked.

"Chores are pretty much caught up here," John replied. "He might just as well learn what has to be done in Quincy now as never."

"John?"

"Yeah, Ma?"

"Are ya up to somethin'?"

"What made you ask that?"

"Ya're all fancied up in your good britches and that new shirt I sewed up for ya last spring," Wilma observed.

"I just took a fancy to wearin' a shirt, Ma," he re-

13

turned. "My shoulders got sunburnt yesterday and I don't want 'em to git any more blistered."

"Comes from workin' without a shirt. Well, I reckon." She stared at John as she poured herself a cup of coffee. She, like Nellie, had learned to rely on her feelings, her intuitions. "Johnny, ya'll be needin' some money, won't ya?"

"I'll git the money for the grain. And we'll carry a lunch with us," John said.

"Well, I see ya got your book out in which ya wrote about your dreams," Wilma commented. "Ya better pack up the resta that fried chicken from last night and git some apples from the cellar. I'll be back directly."

"What's she all upset about?" Tom asked.

"I'll tell you later. Finish your breakfast."

Wilma returned, carrying a small pouch of coins. She put them in John's hand. "Tommy, you go out and put the horses to the wagon."

Tom left.

Wilma put the palm of her hand flat on top of the book in which John had recorded his dreams. "Maybe I didn't do right, son, but I've read what ya got written here. Ya're gonna have to improve on your spellin' some. I caught quite a few misspelled words. But I was able to cipher them out." She motioned for him to put the money in his pocket, pouch and all. "Sam, he don't much like for me to do that, but he knows I'm gonna do it, so he don't say much."

"Do what, Ma?"

"Give ya money like that. He thinks I encourage you boys. Well, maybe I do. He says ya can't run a farm without boys. And I tell him it ain't right for boys to live without women. Sam agrees. So I says to him, 'Sam, ya know ya ain't gonna find no women around here, not even in Fowler.' Your pa don't argue none with me about that." She touched his shoulders. "They don't even feel warm, Johnny. All right, ya go on with ya. But I want to ask ya one thing. If ya ever get to see the ocean—I mean really—will ya sit down on a big rock, stare out at those waves and think real hard about me? Maybe I'll be able to pick up the picture. I've dreamed about the ocean, too."

"Ma—"

"Shh. Go on with ya before your pa gets up," Wilma said understandingly. "And ya be sure ya send Tom right back home. He's not to dally none in Quincy. Tell him I don't want to worry none about him. I'll have enough worryin' on my hands with you."

John put his arms about his mother. "Don't worry, Ma, I'll be all right." He kissed her on the cheek.

John and Tom Collier wore straw hats. The sun was to their backs as they arrived at Quincy. They went directly to the grain market. The wagon was unloaded by midmorning.

The boys ate their lunch in the shade of a large elm tree in the town square and watched the fancy carriages go by. John pointed out the difference between country people and city folks. Then the boys napped until the shade moved to the other side of the tree.

"You'll be goin' back to the farm by yourself, Tom," John said as he gave the boy two dollars. "Just stay on the road marked Fowler and you'll find your way. That way you'll know how to come back next time."

Tom asked the obvious question. John just shook the lad's hand and told him to go on his way.

The wagon looked like a small house on wheels. Brightly painted red with large yellow letters trimmed in white and black, the vehicle could not help but attract attention. The letters spelled out: Dr. Dillsworth's Tonic. It arrived shortly after Tom left. John observed the phenomenon from a distance, still in the shade of the elm tree, enjoying his first sensation of freedom and independence.

Small crowds gathered around the garishly painted wagon. A short plump man with a high stovepipe hat introduced himself as Dr. Homer Dillsworth. He talked fast with a kind of patter that was more confusing than convincing. Finally he extracted a large gold watch from his vest pocket, perspiration streaking down his face, and dangled it before the eyes of the curious.

"Now, my friends, I am going to show you a *remark-able* feat of hypnosis!" the self-proclaimed Dr. Dillsworth declared. "First, I'll ask for a volunteer from the audience. No, not you, madam, I can tell by your stern expression that you are wholeheartedly a disbeliever. Yes, boy, *you*, son. Come up here."

A boy of twelve leaped onto the small platform behind the vehicle.

"I want you to stare at this lovely instrument of time," Homer said in articulate tones. "You're watching closely, are you? Good. Closer. Look closer. Now you're getting sleepy. Very sleepy. Yes, indeed. Very, very sleepy."

The boy closed his eyes and began to snore.

Out of the side of his mouth, Homer whispered, "Don't carry this damn thing too far. No snoring."

The boy ceased snoring.

"Aha! The boy is under hypnosis," Homer announced, his red nose glistening brightly in the afternoon sun. "Hold out your hand, boy. Straight out and rigid." The boy did as he was told. "Now I'm going to stick a pin in your hand and you'll not feel a thing." The boy flinched. "I said you'd *not* feel a thing."

Homer held up a hatpin and started to jab it into the

boy's hand. Someone shrieked. "Ah, madam, I must ask you to refrain from vocalizing during my act—I mean, my demonstration. You see, your piercing high C sharp or was that a D flat—I don't have perfect pitch—has caused this lad's subconscious to recoil in fear. I shall have to employ another device." Out of the side of his mouth he whispered, "This is only a trick. For godsake don't move." Loudly he proclaimed, "I will therefore induce my client to take a swig of Dr. Dillsworth's Tonic, the most miraculous cure of pain this side of the Atlantic Ocean." He opened the bottle and gave the boy a drink. The contents were sweet-tasting and easy to swallow.

"Now, put your hand forward again, boy. Good lad," Homer encouraged. "Instead of using the hatpin—and I must ask you all to keep utter silence—this time I will use a needle, and stick it through the boy's hand, bringing it out the other side." The youth snored. "Not that again, you dolt! Trust me." With extended pinky fingers, Homer put a needle to the underside of the boy's hand. The man's pudgy, nimble fingers were able to maneuver in such a way that he made it appear as if the first needle went in the underside as he brought a second needle out the back of the hand. His movement was so subtle that nobody detected the deceit.

One lady fainted.

The boy half-opened one eye to see that the needle indeed had not gone through his hand. He sighed in relief.

"Now then, my friends," Homer recited, "you have seen the effect of Dr. Dillsworth's Tonic on this boy. He is completely without pain. As for the dear lady who fainted away from a case of nerves, had she been properly fortified with Dr. Dillsworth's Tonic she would not even have had the vapors from watching such a display. Who will buy the first bottle?"

He sold seven bottles.

"Now I will show you one final display of my talents," Homer exclaimed.

A tallish traveling man in a checkered suit had been attracted by the show. Carrying a straw woven satchel, he ambled over to observe Homer about the same time that John Collier got close enough to get a good look.

"My friends, I am about to regress this boy," Homer announced, rolling his syllables, "beyond his past lives as a human being to the time he was a jungle ape. Boy, when I snap my fingers, you will be a jungle ape." He snapped his fingers. "Go into your act, kid," he whispered from the side of his mouth.

The boy began jumping around as he thought an ape should. The audience was impressed.

Homer snapped his fingers. "In five minutes you will revert to your natural boy self again. In the meantime, you will be a dog, a matter of regressing even farther back in time." Again he snapped his fingers and the boy began barking. A few moments later he jumped down from the platform, barking and running like a wild dog around the wagon, then down the street and around the side of the building.

Homer hawked another ten bottles of tonic.

"If there are no more buyers," Homer announced—besides he had run out of full bottles—"that ends our little show for today." He waved to the people as they left, then turned to fan, chuckling amusedly to himself.

John scratched his head before he noticed that he was being observed by the man in the checkered suit.

"Howdy!" The nattily dressed man was friendly. "My name's Clarence Hoskins. Among other things I'm a private detective by trade. Just come down from Rock Island. On my way to St. Louis, but I thought I'd stop off here in Hannibal for a day or two."

"This here's Quincy, mister," John corrected him.

"It is? Well, I'll be switched! I got off at the wrong stop. Don't that beat midnight?" Clarence Hoskins said, slapping his thigh. "Well, guess I'll just have to see what's goin' on in Quincy, won't I? Didn't catch your name, son?"

"John. John Collier."

"You from around here, Johnny?" Hoskins asked.

"Out a ways."

"Can I buy ya a beer?"

"Don't much drink beer," John admitted.

"Best thing to cool ya off on a hot day like this. Must be close to a hundred," stated Clarence.

"A hundred *what?*"

"Degrees. The heat."

"Oh."

"Come on, I'll buy ya a beer someplace."

John held back. "I kinda wanted to talk to that Dr. Dillsworth for a spell, if it's all the same."

"Poor man is probably exhausted from his show. Come have a drink with me and we'll come back to see him when it cools down."

Clarence Hoskins had his free arm about the youth's shoulder, edging him to a nearby saloon.

As Clarence and John entered the Gold Rail saloon, the boy who had run off barking like a dog returned to Homer Dillsworth's wagon to get paid for his acting bit. The plump man gave the boy a round dollar for his efforts and told him not to come back for at least four hours. He could not use the same boy twice in a row, people might catch on.

# CHAPTER TWO

John drank part of one beer and immediately got sick. The saloonkeeper gave him a glass of sweet soda to settle his stomach.

"I never realized ya were so inexperienced at drinkin', boy," Clarence Hoskins said.

"I'm inexperienced about most things."

"I kinda figured that," Clarence remarked. "What ya got in the book there?"

"Oh, just some things I wrote. Nothin' important." John looked into the sudden earnest expression in the man's face. "Have *you* ever seen the ocean?"

"The ocean?" Clarence laughed and ordered a second beer. "Sure I have. Several times. I seen it down in Savannah, Georgia, and up in Boston, Massachusetts. I've even seen the Gulf of Mexico all the way at the end of the Mississippi River."

"You've traveled a lot, haven't you?"

"That's about all I do. My work takes me a lot of different places," Clarence bragged. "Here I was in Chicago a coupla months back. I run into a humdinger of a case there and made me two hundred dollars. That's big money for detective work. It ain't the biggest I ever made. I had this one case up in Boston. I got it when I was down in Savannah and it took me all the way to Boston. A lady by the name of Mrs. Phenwick hired me after I was workin' for her nephew down south."

"Phenwick? I know that name," John said in reaction.

"You do? Well, they wouldn't be the same people," Clarence commented. "They wouldn't come farther west than Massachusetts."

"They own a shipping business?" John questioned.

"How'd you know? I mean, yeah—they do. But we gotta be thinkin' about another Phenwick family—unless you've been in Boston."

"Never."

"There, ya see?"

"Augusta Phenwick?"

"Huh?"

"Was there an Augusta Phenwick?" John asked.

"That name rings somethin'," Clarence replied. "But the lady I worked for was Patricia Phenwick. How'd you know the name?"

"I don't know it," John answered, as befuddled as Clarence appeared to be. "I lived all my life on a farm somwheres between here and Fowler, Illinois. Can't thinka where I heard that name. Reckon it was in some book I read. My ma came from Philadelphia when she was a young'un and she brung—I mean, brought some books with her. I read alla them at least twice."

Clarence stared strangely at the young man. Suddenly he snapped his fingers and pointed at him. "Spell Phenwick."

John scratched his head, rolled his eyes. "P-H-E-N-W-I-C-K."

"Ya said P-H, didn't ya? Not F?"

"Yes. P-H."

"How come?"

"Well, seems to me that's just the way you'd spell it."

"Say, ya got any money on ya?" Clarence asked ten minutes later, after he had drunk a third glass of beer.

John sat for a moment and figured. "Well, maybe around five dollars at the most," he contrived. He had been warned about sharp operators on other occasions when he had been in Quincy. His brother Lemuel had had a run-in with a slicker one who taught him how to gamble. Lemuel lost all the money he had. His pa gave him a whipping when he got home. John would never forget that. He had the bulk of his money tucked away.

"Look, kid, I hope ya kin thinka me as your friend. I know ya don't know me none," Clarence said. "And I'll admit when I seen ya I thought ya looked like a soft touch. But if ya only got five dollars—well, I wouldn't wanta try no funny stuff with ya."

"What're you gettin' at, Mr. Hoskins?"

"Call me Clarence, Johnny." He wiped the back of his hand across his mouth. "Ya remember that man we was watchin', the medicine man?"

"What about him?"

"Did ya see him hypnotize that kid?"

"I never put much stock in that," John remarked. "I seen that kinda thing happen before. He pays those boys to act like they're hypnotized. I read a book about hypnotism once. It was originally written in German and translated into American—I mean, English. You see, I'm mostly self-taught and I don't always git my English right—but I'm workin' on it."

"Yeah, well, I seen a woman in Chicago get hypnotized, and it was for real," Clarence explained. "At first I thought it was the usual trick. She got all stiff and two guys laid her flat as a board across the backsa two chairs and another guy got up and sat on her stomach. She never budged an inch. Well, then this guy what was hypnotizin' her, he started talkin' to her. And she began talkin' like a little girl, tellin' about things that happened when she was a kid. Her people were killed by Injuns. Well, if that weren't enough to curl my hair, she started tellin' what it was like before she was born. She remembered about pickin' what parents she would have and stuff like that. Then she remembered bein' someone else in a life before this one. I tell ya, I plum got the willies and got all creepy-feelin' up and down my back."

"I swan. You don't mean it!" John said, a tremble of excitement going through him. "You don't suppose—"

"I don't know what to suppose," Clarence cut in. "But I'll tell ya this, I sure done a lotta thinkin' 'bout that. I talked to the woman later and she never remembered a thing about it. She was a good Christian lady, too. She was pretty shook up when she heard tell what she had said."

John sneezed. "Excuse me."

"Bless ya."

"I always sneeze when I get a whiffa violets like that," John said, wiping his nose with a red handkerchief.

"Violets like *what?* I don't smell nuthin'," Clarence stated.

"I thought I smelled violets," John said. "Somethin' sure made me sneeze. Fact is, I know perfectly well they were violets. I'd know the smell anywhere. When somethin' like that makes you sneeze, you stand cleara it. Like the fella says, don't go pettin' the lions if you're not a lion-tamer."

Clarence laughed. "That made me thinka Harriet Pettijohn; she was the girl I was hired to look after in Boston. She later married one-a them Phenwick boys. She used to think she smelled violets ever' so often. I'd tell her it was just her imagination playin' tricks on her. I never could smell any, and usually I got a pretty good sense-a smell. Anyway, what I was about to say a while back, why don't we go over and talk to that Doc Dillsworth and see if he really does know how to hypnotize people? We'll offer him a dollar to see if he kin put you under. That is if ya don't mind turnin' loose-a a dollar. I'll take somethin' to write on and mark down what ya say—if ya kin be hypnotized."

"Well, I don't know. A dollar's a lot of money," John said, "and I haven't got but five."

About sundown, Clarence and John hiked a short distance out of town to where they were told Doc Dillsworth usually camped for the night. The people of Quincy were particular about him sleeping right in the center of town with his horse grazing on the grass in the square. The spot was down by the river near a small stream that trickled into the muddy water. The stream was spring-fed and crystal-clear.

Homer Dillsworth had removed his costume, clad only in his trousers when the men came upon him. Modesty forced him to pull into a shirt. "Had you fellas come ten minutes sooner, you would have seen the entire of Homer Dillsworth exposed. Not a particularly colorful sight. What brings you here? No handouts. Can't afford to feed every tramp along the way."

"We've done et, Doc, thank ya anyway," Clarence said. "We was wantin' to talk to ya."

"I usually don't give interviews this time of the day, gentlemen," the older man said. "I've got my evening chores to perform—bottles to fill. Going to have to see if

I can't pick up some more in St. Louis. I'm beginning to run low. Business has been pretty good. I oughta hire that one boy, he's a good little shill. Had a kid traveling with me for about a year. Good boy, too. Alas."

"Mr. Dillsworth," John began.

"That's *Doctor* Dillsworth. Homer P.," Dillsworth explained.

"Yes, Dr. Dillsworth," John started again. "Did you really hypnotize that boy?"

"I—uh—why—uh—yes, of course," Dillsworth replied. "Hey, you're not accusing me of chicanery, are you?"

"No, I don't think I am."

"What my friend is wonderin', Doc," Clarence interrupted, "is if ya're really a professional hypnotist. Ya see, I'm a private detective and I—"

"Oh—uh—private—what—uh—detective, is it?" Homer was flustered.

Taking advantage of the man's fear of the law, Clarence took a new line of approach. "We actually would like to see if ya kin put a person under hypno—whatever ya call it."

"Hypnotism?" Homer straightened, became indignant. "I'll have you know I learned all my professional skills from a very fine magician. Barnaby the Great was his name. Magnificent! I was just a struggling young actor, singer and occasionally a dancer when I met Barnaby. We played on the same—well, at the same theater—uh—in Europe."

"Oh, you really have traveled around, haven't you, Doc?" John exclaimed admiringly.

"Why—uh—yes—ye-us." Homer realized he had at least one gullible member in his immediate audience.

Clarence related about the hypnotism incident he had witnessed in Chicago. "So we was wonderin' if ya might be able to put Johnny here under like that."

"For what reason?" questioned Homer, some doubts rising in his mind.

"Because I've been having very strange dreams ever since I was a little boy," John explained. "I've always wondered why I could see the ocean so clearly in my dreams, yet I've never actually seen any ocean. And there are other things. We'll give you a whole dollar if you'll try it. Even if you can't make me unconscious, we'll give you a dollar just for tryin'.'"

"Can't beat that offer, can I?" Homer snorted. "Very well. For this occasion, however, I'll find old Barnaby's crystal pendulum. I'll just be a few minutes. There's a blanket there. Spread it out on the grass and lie down, Johnny. I'll be right back." He disappeared into his wagon.

John was reclining comfortably on the blanket when Homer reappeared, wearing a purple robe with silver stars and moons on it. The garment fit him tightly, obviously a relic from the lamented Barnaby. He carried the many-prismed crystal dangling on a silver chain.

"Now, Johnny, I want you just to stare at this crystal," Homer said, as he swayed it gently before his eyes, "and feel yourself getting sleepier and sleepier."

Johnny yawned. His eyes were fastened on the crystal. Homer exchanged glances with Clarence. The youth's eyes were soon closed and he gave all indications of being in a trance.

"It's ten years ago, Johnny," Homer droned in a monotonous voice. "Do you know where you are?"

"I'm down on the farm, tendin' to the plowin'," John returned, his voice dry and expressionless. "It's a hot one today."

"All right, Johnny," Homer interrupted, "it's now twenty years ago. Where are you?"

27

"I'm just a little fella. Can't even talk yet. Nellie—she's just a baby," Johnny replied.

"Write that down," Homer whispered to Clarence, trying to control his excitement. "All right, Johnny, it's now thirty years ago. Where are you?"

"I'm in the ether," Johnny answered after several moments' pause. "I'm so free and just floatin' about."

"Are you by yourself?"

"No, my friend is here. He was waitin' for me when I came over."

"*He*? What's his name?" Homer questioned.

"It's not really he," Johnny returned. "Over here there's no male or female. I mean, there are. I saw my sister the other day—Margaret."

"Your sister's name is Margaret? I thought you told us your sister's name is Nellie."

"Nellie isn't my sister yet—not again. She was a long time ago. I can't remember when. She wasn't my sister when Margaret was," Johnny explained. "It's all very confusing. I'm aware of others who have been related to me in the past."

"All right, Johnny," Homer said, when the lad fell silent. "It is now forty years ago. Forty years ago, do you understand?"

"Yes."

"Where are you now, Johnny?" Homer questioned.

"Johnny? You must have me confused. You *are* speaking to me, aren't you?" the voice questioned from Johnny's mouth. It had changed and sounded older. "Johnny lives in Portland."

"Where do you live?" inquired Homer.

"In Greenfield. Johnny is a doctor. He comes once in a while."

"Greenfield? Greenfield, Illinois?"

"No, no." A slight chuckle. "Greenfield, Maine."

"The state-a Maine?" questioned Clarence, scribbling as fast as he could.

"It used to be Massachusetts territory when we first came to Greenfield," the hypnotized youth said.

"Is Margaret with you?" Homer ventured to ask.

"No. No, Titter died in the fire with Rachel."

"Titter?"

"That is what we called Margaret when she was a girl."

"Who is Rachel?"

"Titter's daughter and"—a pause—"*his*." Again silence.

"Who *is* there with you?"

"My mother comes to see me. She likes the cottage I built on the sea cliff." Still the voice of an older man.

"What is your name?"

"Michael."

"Michael?" Homer glanced at Clarence. "Michael *who?*"

Contemplative stillness. "I just remember Michael O."

"Is your friend there?" Homer quizzed.

"Danny? No, I haven't seen him in some time. He doesn't come to Greenfield too often now that Titter is gone. It pains him very much. He won't go in the old house. Titter thought it was haunted, but I've been in it several times and I've never seen any sign of any haunting."

Clarence whispered, "Can I ask him a question?"

"Go ahead."

"Do you know Patricia Phenwick?" Clarence asked.

"I know of her," was the reply after several moments of consideration. "She married Edward. I've seen her. Yes. We've met."

"Who was Augusta?" Clarence continued.

Long silence. Clarence was about to ask the question again when John turned his head from side to side. "She wouldn't adopt me. I wanted to be *his* brother. I never could understand that. She seemed to like me all right, even when she didn't like Titter. I don't want to remember."

"Johnny," Homer said softly as if he knew what he was doing, "it is now a hundred years ago, Johnny. Where are you?"

"I'm in the ether again. I've been here a long time." His voice sounded still different, very far away.

"Is your friend with you?"

"My friend? Oh, you mean my soul mate? Yes, we're together often. We're learning much. We've been told— and don't ask me who said it, I don't know—that we're going to be born into two consecutive lives together. We have things we must learn in each."

"There in that ether are you men or women?" asked Homer.

"We're neither ... and we're both," the words came from John's mouth.

"Is your name still Michael?"

"No ... I have no name." John began twisting, his body contorting spastically.

"Johnny ... Johnny ... listen to me," Homer said, trying not to sound panicky. "It is just thirty years ago again. Do you hear me?"

John appeared less restless, but his muscles twitched. "Yes. I hear you. Michael is dead and I'm between lives."

"Good." Homer sighed as he glanced at Clarence. "I hope you've got this all down."

"Most of it," Clarence affirmed.

"I hope so, too," John commented. "I need to know this information."

"Why?"

"So I can find my soul mate again." Silence.

"It is now just ten years ago, Johnny." Pause. "Can you hear me, Johnny?"

"Yes."

"Now you're coming up to the present time," Homer announced. He gave posthypnotic suggestions that John would feel fine and not have any physical aftereffects from the session. "Barnaby always used to say that before he would bring someone out of it."

A few minutes later, John Collier blinked his eyes open. He glanced up at Clarence, then at Homer. An embarrassed grin. "Well, I reckon it didn't work after all, did it?" He fished in his pocket to find a dollar to give Homer. "A promise is a promise."

# CHAPTER THREE

For as long as Kate could remember, she had never been happy at Phenwick House. Her discontent stemmed from an uncomfortable feeling that came over her whenever she was alone in the old mansion on the seacoast at Greenfield, Maine. What ominous gloom hung over that structure? Dark memories still lingered there. She knew only too well that it was the death place of Augusta Phenwick.

Kate Phenwick Cathcart was born on July 12, 1835, the daughter of Rebecca Phenwick and Robert Cathcart. She had been a pretty child with rosy cheeks and golden brown hair that got darker as she grew older. Her eyes were lilac-colored, often as circular as her face was round. A thin, finely shaped nose. A defiant chin with a dimple in it. Of medium height, her all-over body shape was roundish but not plump, at least not in early years. Like her mother before her, she was an excellent horsewoman. An avid swimmer, she spent most of her summers, particularly as a child, in the ocean or in the pond beyond the house wher she could swim as well as any boy in the entire village of Greenfield. Those lilac eyes seemed to glisten with adventure and enthusiasm for life. Yet there were times when a kind of winsome fretfulness appeared in them. It was that fear she had felt of Phenwick House. No matter how she tried to set her mind, the apprehension was always there: silent, ominous, as if some unseen force were stalking her.

Often she stood in the large sitting room, staring at the imposing portrait of Augusta Phenwick that had been painted and artistically signed by the artist, Clayton Latshaw. Many others of Latshaw's works hung in the mansion from the era of Augusta Phenwick—relatives, friends. Perhaps her favorite was that of old Ben Strothart, Augusta's uncle, and the true founder, albeit from piracy, of the Phenwick fortune. That likeness hung in the second-floor hallway.

Robert Cathcart had been dead for nearly six years. His widow, Rebecca, had never remarried, nor had she any inclination to do so. She was content raising her one child, living in that remote part of the world where civilization was just beginning to raise its head with the coming of the mills. She rode daily, when the weather permitted, and, like her daughter, swam in the summertime. Long walks, meditatively through the forests, around the village that was building and expanding beyond the boundaries of the precise Phenwick property. The entire piece of land had had at one time been Phenwick property, acquired by Augusta when she first settled in the area. They still owned much of the land in outlying areas. As people moved in, they had sold plots of acreage, put in roads and allowed the village of

Greenfield to develop around the town square, the park with the gazebo in it.

Time had etched itself well into Rebecca Phenwick's face. She had never been the beauty that her half sister Susannah had been, nor did she have the immense talent. Neither did she have the ambition for notoriety and acclaim. She was the quiet Phenwick woman, the one content with country living, preferring to be away from the bustling cities. She loved the serenity of being among the pines and maple trees, the oaks and the elms, where the winters were long and the summers relatively short, the springs were gloriously radiant and the autumns were painted with such vibrant colors that one could not but stand in awe of the majestic beauty.

A few livestock were still kept on the large sprawling estate, mostly horses. A couple of cows. Chickens that pecked around the house and barn. Rebecca liked to have her own vegetable garden. The fruit orchard still bore many apples and pears, peaches in the summertime. The household staff included Cora Beaton, the housekeeper, a close and dear friend; a cook; a handyman; and one male servant in the house, as well as a cleaning maid who came in by the day. Rebecca liked to run the house as if it indeed were a farm. She liked to put up preserves, enlisting the assistance of the servants. With her own sleeves rolled up, she was in the middle superintending and as busy as the rest. Kate, too, helped in that project. The cellar was filled with apples, pears, squash, pumpkins, cabbage, other vegetables that would keep into the winter months. Rebecca liked to feel herself close to the soil. An earthy person, she was the antithesis of her mother, the wildly eccentric Patricia Phenwick of Boston, who for the most part ignored her second daughter's existence.

Ella Shane had long been governess and friend to Kate.

She had been hired into service shortly after Kate was born, taking the load of raising the child from Rebecca, who was not particularly the motherly sort. The mother dearly loved her daughter, whom she always called Kate Phenwick, when the rest of Greenfield merely called her Kate.

The governess was a woman in her late thirties, who had never married. Ella Shane was a proud creature. At one time she had been jilted by an intended husband. She never truly got over that heartbreak, nor did she show a marked interest in men again. A sturdy woman, she tended toward being stout, with large hips and a significant bosom. Plain-faced with a long nose, she pulled her hair severely back on her head. Having come from a good family, she had a proper education, therefore acted as tutor for young Kate.

As civilization more and more approached Greenfield, a school was established. Rebecca wanted her daughter to associate with the other children of the community. Ella then became a guide for the girl, helping her with the long hours of study, learning as much or more than the child and enjoying the opportunity. A happy woman, she never complained about her lot, nor did she show any discontent with her position. She had become a good friend of Rebecca's; although there was a time several years before when Robert Cathcart, the quiet unassuming sea captain, had seemed to cast romantic glances at the young governess. A passing fancy at best. Ella forgave herself for entertaining such thoughts about a married man. Rebecca never spoke of the matter. It was over and done with. She knew her seagoing husband was an adventurer in his quiet way, that he had had many experiences. In her way of thinking, that was a man's prerogative as long as he was good to his wife and family.

Kate had deeply loved her father. He was often away many months. Upon returning, he was practically a stranger to her when she was a small child. With the years, after his retirement, she became much closer to the man. She did not completely understand him, nor his strange desire to have spent so much time at sea. Was he given to melancholia? That could well have been the case, for there were times when Kate felt herself a bit atrabilious.

Devoted Osgood Wymer had long been the handyman about Phenwick House. He drove the carriage and saw to taking Kate back and forth to school. He had become a masculine figure who shared her enthusiasm for the changing events during her growing-up years. Osgood was a merry sort with no particularly distinguishing features. Balding, he was thin and slightly bent from years of working in the garden and tending to the animals. A good man, he read his Bible every day. Living in the old O'Plaggerty cottage on the estate, he took his meals with the other servants at the house. He liked the solitude of having his own place.

Osgood had always been a kind of second father in Kate's mind, although he was nothing like Captain Cathcart. His duty was to meet Kate daily at the schoolhouse, located on the town square. The school building had twice been added on to, and still was not large enough to accommodate the increasing number of children who populated Greenfield. He was known to most of the young people, notorious for his farfetched tales and yarns, little pranks and sense of humor.

Osgood had seen the slowly developing relationship coming between Kate and Ronald Boggs. The Boggses were a family who had lived several generations in Greenfield, brought there by Augusta. Ronald had dark straggly hair, devilment gleamed in his brown eyes. Not good-looking, he emitted a pervading sensuality, particularly as he reached his late teens. That characteristic had a magnetic attraction for many of the young ladies of Greenfield, which made him extremely popular.

When it was discovered that Kate was more than casually impressed by Ronald Boggs, his parents set about to encourage the boy to pursue the Phenwick heiress' attention.

Ronald was athletically built, always jumping about overenergetically. It seemed as if he were dancing or presenting himself in a provocative posture.

Kate's best girl friend was Patsy O'Plaggerty. Patsy's father, James, has established the Shamrock Tavern on the town square. She was the quintessence of femininity, flirtatious ways and distant Irish beauty. Red hair. Sparkling green eyes. There were times when Kate became a bit envious of Patsy's ability to attract the interest of the boys.

Kate's second best friend was Fanny Mockerty, one of several children. She did not possess the beauty of either Kate or Patsy. But she had an outgoing personality that made her extremely sought after among her peers. She was perhaps more sincere in her loyalty than Patsy, never flounting her female charms. Where Patsy had wild, curly hair, Fanny's was straight, which she wore in a pigtail. She was cute in her way, the boys noticed her.

Perhaps the least-liked girl in that age group was Alice Mumford, who, although Kate was unaware of the fact, was distantly related to her through her grandfather. Alice, too, was pretty except for rather large teeth that detracted from her appearance. She laughed loudly and was well known about town because she was the grandniece of Grace Mumford, owner of the general store. Her brother Tom was two years older. He was considered somewhat of a bully by the other children because he was constantly asserting himself. He and Ronald Boggs were sometimes chums. Whenever Ronald was involved with Tom, they usually managed to get into trouble. Consequently the Boggses had forbidden Ronald to associate with the Mumford boy.

By the time Kate reached eighteen, she believed that she was madly in love with Ronald. She had graduated that June, which was more than most girls in Greenfield did. Because of their association during graduation, Ronald continued seeing Kate on a regular basis. Often on the weekend, he would come calling in a shay and ask to take her riding on the Portland road, or through the forest past the old Indian camp, or on the old country road that went by the textile mill where he worked to the other side of Boggs Creek. Kate was at the age and inclination where she was easily impressed by a young man's closeness. She could be falling under influence and persuasion. That particular late spring evening when they rode up beyond Boggs Creek and the textile mill, a feeling of anticipation came over the girl as she sensed that Ronald's motivation was peculiar. He acted differently than he usually did. He whistled a lot and laughed for no particular reason.

"What strikes you so funny, Ronald?" asked Kate as she sat on the seat beside him in the slowly moving, rattling shay.

"Anticipation," Ronald replied. "I'm thinkin' about what's gonna happen and how much fun it's gonna be."

"What *is* going to happen?"

"You'll see in good time."

Suddenly a feeling of apprehension came over the girl. She tried to stare into the dark face of the youth. "You don't seem yourself tonight. Have you been up to something?"

"I've brought me a bottle of gin along," Ronald boasted. "I've already drunk at least a quarter of it. I'm feelin' very good."

"Gin? Where did you get gin?"

"Tom Mumford got it for me from his aunt's store. Do you want some?"

"No." The very thought of liquor made Kate react with a terrible queasy feeling. She could barely tolerate the smell of it.

"Why not? There's a little chill in the air. It will warm you up."

"I'm not cold, Ronald."

"Glad to hear that. I was hopin' you would be plenty warm tonight, Katie."

"What do you have in mind?"

"A little fun," Ronald said with more laughter. "We'll go up a ways where there's an old cabin that used to belong to my uncle. Nobody's there now. The floor is rotted in places and the roof leaks. We can be by ourselves and undisturbed."

"Ronald . . . what are thinking?" Kate asked after they drove a short distant farther. In the static silence, her feeling of apprehension had increased.

"I'm thinkin' it's time you and I were actin' like a man and woman should act," Ronald replied, reaching over and putting his hand on her leg. He squeezed tightly.

Kate gently eased his hand away. "I think it might not be a good idea for us to go any farther up the lane. Perhaps you'd better take me back."

"I thought you were in love with me," Ronald stated.

"I do like you very much," Kate answered. "I think maybe I am in love with you."

"You just think—you're not certain?" Ronald laughed. "Well, after tonight you'll be convinced, I have no doubt of that. Then we'll have many other good times together. Know what I mean, Kate?"

"I'm afraid I do know what you mean and I don't know that I want to experience what you have in mind. Not now. If you love me, if you want to marry me, then why don't you ask me? I certainly don't want to go to some terrible little cabin in the woods and give myself to you."

"And what if I take what I want," Ronald asked. "You know a man gets a few drinks and he has a lot of strength and desire, and he doesn't like to have his wants turned down."

"In that case, before you take another swig or get any further desires, I insist you turn this shay around and we go back. You can take me home, Ronald Boggs. That's final!"

"Oh, no, Kate, it isn't. You and I are going to have a time of it, we are." He held the bottle to his lips and took several large swallows.

Seeing moonlight reflecting as it hit the glass, Kate took a desperate measure. With all her strength, she knocked the bottle from his hand. It fell to the ground. He swore. Stopping the horses, he quickly scampered down to retrieve the bottle.

"Now see what you've done, you damn fool! The bottle is nearly empty."

"That's too bad, Ronald Boggs." With that she grabbed the reins and shook them for the horses to start.

"Come back, come back, you fool!" Ronald screamed.

With Phenwick determination, Kate continued to drive up the road, knowing that there was a cutoff she could take so she would not have to return that way. If she could move the horse fast enough, she would be able to escape before Ronald could dash through the woods and meet her on the other side.

She drove with a fury. Twigs whipped past her. The horse had not been driven like that that evening. A well-spirited beast, he was ready for a run. Finding the right turnoff from distant memory, she guided the horse and managed to get past the spot Ronald was approaching, screaming at the top of his lungs. His profanity was vile, words that she had never heard before. Fortunately they were muffled in the echo of the forest.

Reaching the town square, Kate raced the horse through the quiet streets around to Old Main Street and the side road that cut off, leading to the Phenwick cottages. Pulling up at the gate to Osgood Wymer's house, she barely wrapped the reins around a post and ran to the door. Osgood had been asleep. She gave instructions that he was to saddle two horses and lead one behind him as she took the shay back to the Boggses' house near the textile mill.

Osgood helped her onto the horse at the Boggses' place. Assured she was in place, he asked if she was ready.

"Yes. But I want to ride back by Mill Road, through the old Indian camp, and come that way to the house."

"That's the long way, Miss Kate."

"I know it is. I need to ride hard to get anger from me," the girl replied. "I want you to come with me. You don't mind, do you, Osgood?"

"No, Miss Kate. I've had me a nap," Osgood said understandingly.

An hour or so later Kate lay awake in her room. Moonlight fell in through the window. Her heart was deeply troubled. It would have been so easy for her to have submitted to Ronald Boggs's wishes. She rationalized that she did love the boy. But did she love him *that* much? Even if she did and had allowed him to have his way, would she have respect for herself and for him afterward? Or would she feel as if she had committed a sin, and be plagued with a bitter memory that would haunt her the rest of her life?

# CHAPTER FOUR

Matronly Lydia Ornby, Rebecca's foster-daughter, lived at Phenwick House. She was the quiet spinster, who had become scattered with the years, realizing that no man wanted her as a wife. She had part of her father's inheritance, which was a sizable amount because he was second-generation Phenwick. Her wealth had not attracted suitable men to her. Several times she had been in love, she thought, but something had always occurred to alter the course of what she believed to be true love. Time had embittered her. She projected a dismal, pessimistic outlook that saw the dark side of conditions.

Often Lydia visited the Shamrock Tavern. She was known to many of the men of low character in town with whom she drank. A lady was never seen in such an establishment. Women of low moral standards were. If Rebecca Phenwick Cathcart did not approve of Lydia's behavior, then Lydia would take a house in town of her own, which she had done three times before. Always out of loneliness she had returned to Phenwick House, begging to be understood by her foster-mother.

Lydia always slept late in the morning, long after the regular activity of Phenwick House was well under way. Rebecca tolerated Lydia's habits, knowing in her heart that Lydia was truly an unhappy woman. It saddened her to see Lydia destroying herself, for she was but a few years younger than Rebecca. Lydia was never convinced that virtue was worth cultivating. Besides, wasn't it too late?

Kate tried to be sympathetic toward her stepsister. She had long heard of Lydia's reputation. It was common gossip, even among the younger people. Perhaps it was because of Lydia's notoriety that Ronald Boggs thought he could get familiar with Kate.

Ella Shane had gone to the village to get some thread at the new general store, which had been moved from Old Main Street into a newer, larger building on the square. With the death of her sister, Alma, Grace Mumford had enlarged the store and taken on several employees. The town had become large enough to warrant it. Grace was always a central telegraphing point of gossip and information, particularly of an unsavory nature. The old woman lived vicariously through the excitement that generated through Greenfield. Often she was known to instigate a rumor or two just to liven things up a bit. After his disastrous night with Kate Cathcart, Ronald Boggs managed to get word to Grace Mumford that intimate things had occurred between Kate and himself, after which she had become angered and left him stranded in the forest. Grace could hardly wait to telegraph that bit of information about the village without checking the authenticity of it. Scandal about the Phenwicks was difficult to come by other than that concerning Lydia Ornby. Consequently it was the juiciest item that could be spread. Soon all of Greenfield knew of that night according to Ronald Boggs.

Like Rebecca, Ella Shane called Kate by her first and middle name, a practice the girl's mother had begun from the child's infancy. "Kate Phenwick," Ella exclaimed as she all but ran up the stairs to the girl's room. "Are you there, Kate Phenwick?" She gasped for breath.

Kate appeared at the door to her room. She had been morbidly inconsolable ever since she had received word that gossip had been spread about Ronald Boggs and her. She stayed much to her room, even abiding there when her mother would go out riding and she knew the house was virtually empty. "What is it, Ella?"

"Well, they're changing their song about you now," the governess said.

"What do you mean?" asked Kate, going to the woman to help her to a large rocking chair in the sitting room of her suite.

"News is all over town. Ronald Boggs has eloped with Alice Mumford."

"Ronald? And Alice?" A stab of hurt went through the girl's heart. Although she had been disappointed by Ronald, she had hoped that there might be a reconciliation and that he would come asking her to forgive him for his actions on that night, using the liquor as an excuse for his behavior. "I can't believe it."

"Well, it's true," Ella Shane explained. "I got it directly from Grace Mumford. If anyone knows, she does. Fact of the matter is, not only has he run off with Alice, saying they were going to Bar Harbor where he has a job waiting with his uncle, but he has left a trail of other broken hearts in Greenfield. It seems that Molly Murdock is with child. That child belongs to Ronald."

"I can't believe it."

"How can you not believe it the way he treated you?"

"Ronald and I were very close. I thought I was in love with him. I thought he loved me," Kate responded, tears coming to her voice. "Oh, Ella, what will I do?"

"Pray and thank your lucky stars that you're not in the same condition as Molly Murdock, nor that you got a man such as Ronald Boggs now that you know the type of person he is."

"But the love I felt for him . . ."

"Love? Did you really love him, Kate Phenwick? I wonder. Or was it just an infatuation? We ladies all go through periods when men are extremely romantic and we presume too much, believing sincerity because we want to and don't desire to see the deceit behind the words."

"Was I so foolish, Ella? I don't believe that I could be such a poor judge of human nature. Yet I guess it is true. I wanted to love Ronald. I wanted him to love me. Even that night, had he not had the gin, I might have gone— but of course I didn't."

"Saints be praised that you didn't!" Ella Shane exclaimed. "I'm relieved in my heart to know that you were spared that ordeal. It is too easy for young ladies to succumb to the charms of outrageous scoundrels who selfishly want their own ways in matters, especially pertaining to emotions and physical desires. I'm so very, very pleased that you didn't submit to him."

Kate began to cry, her eyes overflowing with tears as she went to hug Ella. She put her cheek to the woman's large bosom and cried until the dress became damp.

"There, there, Kate Phenwick. You cry all you like. There may be many other tears over men. I pray that is not so, and that the right man for you will appear and you will find happiness. Oh yes, Kate Phenwick, I pray that you will love and be loved in such an all-consuming way that happiness is the story of your life."

Although Ella Shane had been raised a Catholic, she converted to Protestantism when she went to work for Rebecca Cathcart. In those days there had been no Catholic church in Greenfield. Now one had been built, since several Irish emigrant families demanded that their native religion be established. After the church had been erected and the few devout members had become active in their parish, Ella remained a Unitarian, regularly attending services with Rebecca. Wednesday night was always an occasion for the two women, who were involved in their religious life. The church was the center of their activities, both social and otherwise. Rebecca had become extremely enthusiastic about Christianity after the death of Robert Cathcart. While Kate was not rebellious against the church in any way, she lacked the zeal her mother and Ella Shane possessed. Consequently Kate was not that avid in her attendance except on Sunday mornings and evenings.

Wednesday night prayer meeting and services that followed bored Kate. She found them too emotional and, frankly, time-consuming. Usually on such occasions, she would spend the evening with a friend, going when her mother and governess went to church. Occasionally a friend would come and visit with her.

That evening Fanny Mockerty had arranged to visit Phenwick House, to spend time with Kate. The girls planned to walk along the seashore that long summer evening and return to the house by nightfall; then Fanny would wait until the women returned from church.

Cora Beaton, the housekeeper, also attended church on Wednesday night, along with Caspar Riddle, the principal male servant of the house. They went in a separate carriage and sat in a different part of the church than did their employer.

Rebecca left for the meeting. The others departed shortly after. Kate found herself in a situation she did not like, being alone at Phenwick House. It did not occur to her for some time that she was in the old mansion by herself until she became aware that there were no sounds except for the natural creaking noises of the old woodwork. A dart of fear came automatically upon that awareness. What was there about that house that so frightened her when she was alone in it? Was it simply the idea of being alone in such a monstrous old place that for nearly a century had housed Phenwicks? Or was it truly haunted, as some of the children in the village had often suggested? Tales had been carried about the house, particularly from a generation or so back when a woman was said to have been driven mad in it.

Kate kept to her room for several minutes in absolute silence, listening, straining her hearing for the tiniest noise. A breeze blew in through the window, throwing the curtains into the room. It startled her. She left that place and went to the head of the stairs where she gazed into the stern but gentle expression in the painting of Ben Strothart. Often she had studied that kindly, enigmatic face, wondering just what sort of man he had been. Legend had it that he had been a pirate. That was difficult to believe. He did not look like a rough and powerful man of the sea. She could not decide what she thought he must have been like precisely.

Since Fanny usually came the back way, Kate decided to go wait by the barn behind the house. There was a bench. She could sit and listen to the birds as they chattered in the evening in the nearby forest. As she reached the bottom of the stairs, she had a singular impulse to look into the sitting room. Had she heard a sound come from there? Probably not. She pushed the door open stealthily as if expecting to find someone waiting. The room was dimly lit. The large portrait of Augusta Phenwick always seemed imposing. The eyes stared at a person no matter where he was in the room. The expression on the canvas was not unpleasant. Yet a kind of menacing projected from it, as though the lady were watching the occupants of the house she had built.

Kate quickly looked away as trembles of fear went through her. Why should she be frightened of Augusta Phenwick? She had long since been dead. Yet, as she closed the door behind her, she caught a very faint aroma of violets. It was not the first time the fragrance of violets permeated about her or seemed to ride on the breeze, to appear and disappear in a matter of moments when no violets were anywhere to be found.

In her excitement, she went across the hall into the study, a chamber which she rarely entered. It had an even more foreboding atmosphere to it. It had been where her father had spent many long hours, reading and going over maps and charts. Even when Robert Cathcart was living, Kate had had trepidations about going into that room. She did not know precisely why she had such sensations of apprehension about a single room. Always at Phenwick House she had a feeling of mystery as if unseen forces were lingering about, waiting to pounce upon her, or at least to distract her in some way.

She hesitated just inside the door as her eyes met the eyes in the portrait of Daniel Phenwick, Augusta's son. He had been a handsome young man as Clayton Latshaw had captured his likeness on the canvas. Reddish brown hair. Eyes that were lavender. The expression he wore, while smiling, looked just a little forced, as though behind that happiness was a solemn nature. His features were extremely handsome. He was clad in a ruffled blouse with a light blue coat.

As' Kate observed the painting, something happened inside her. Was it a sob that had gurgled from within her soul? Or was it a reaction to the expression she saw, the sadness that seemed to be in his eyes? She could not stand to examine the portrait at any length. Perhaps that painting was the reason she did not often enter the study. The longer she gazed at it the more uneasy she became and the greater her anxiety grew.

Urgency came over her. Were the walls collapsing on her, the ceiling falling? What sort of madness was about to happen? She was certain it was only a matter of moments before some terrible thing would occur if she did not escape.

Kate was trembling when she got outside the house. In her anxiety, she ran as fast as she could go around to the far side of the barn, not stopping until she reached her destination. She leaned against the building, gasping for breath. She had the sensation that she had been chased by a ghost, haunted by an unknown fear.

She had no more than begun breathing with less effort than she saw Fanny Mockerty approaching. Not wanting to wait, she ran to greet her friend. She called for Fanny to remain where she was; Kate would join her and they would go another way to the seashore.

As the girls came together, Kate had gathered her wits and was her usual jovial self. Turning back, she got one final glimpse of the old house. She tried to forget the fear that had almost overwhelmed her moments before. Taking Fanny's hand, she dragged her toward the path that led by the sea cottage on the cliff.

# CHAPTER FIVE

1854

"Kate Phenwick," Rebecca called one day that spring after watching her daughter moping listlessly about, wandering through the garden and down by the old family cemetery. "Kate Phenwick, come here!"

Kate turned to witness her mother standing at the side of Phenwick House. The woman had a freshly gathered bouquet of lilacs which she was preparing to take indoors. "What is it, Mother?" the girl asked as she went to where the other was standing.

"Kate Phenwick, I don't know what's come over you. I would guess it was spring fever, except you've had it all winter. You've carried on like a sick child. I swear I'll have to have the doctor come and look at you."

"I'm all right, Mother. I just don't feel much like being excited about anything," Kate returned with a sigh.

"It's spring, my dear. Just look at these lilacs," Rebecca suggested. "Why don't you gather a bouquet of daffodils for the table? That will brighten your spirits. Daffodils have a way of cheering a person."

"I don't think even daffodils could help, Mother." Kate leaned against a birch tree and stared wistfully into her mother's beautifully charactered face.

"Are you still disturbed over Ronald Boggs?" questioned Rebecca as she examined the lilacs and picked bad leaves from them.

"I don't think it's really Ronald anymore, Mother," Kate said, "not since he's run off to Bar Harbor with Alice Mumford. I've gotten over that."

"Kate Phenwick, there's doubt in your mind, I can tell by the way you speak."

"The thing that is so upsetting is that Ronald left behind him a trail of other broken hearts. He promised many girls many things."

"That Ronald Boggs was a bad one," Rebecca remarked. "That kind spring up all over. It's not just in the big cities. We get them here in the country, too. I've been right friendly with some of the Boggs girls over the years, but the boys have always had that wild, recklessly physical nature. They think themselves bees who can indiscriminately go about pollinating flowers. Well, Kate Phenwick, I shan't say I hope you've learned a lesson. How were you to know about such men as Ronald? You're young and inexperienced. Your stepsister Lydia is planning to go to Portland next week. I was wondering if you would like to go with her."

"To Portland?" A flicker of enthusiasm lit Kate's face, bringing a loveliness that had been quietly dormant over the last few months.

"She's going to see her grandmother, old Aunt Jane. I haven't see her in a good many years," Rebecca commented. "I don't know that I want to see her as age takes over. She was always such a sweet lady. I want to remember her that way—not shriveled up and decrepit."

"Aunt Jane Ornby," Kate whispered. "I don't recall the last time I saw her either. Probably not since I was a little girl. I remember Falmouth House. It frightened me."

"Strange how old houses frighten you. I know you're not comfortable at Phenwick House, but it is the only one we have. When we went to Edward House in Boston, again you had that ominous feeling of apprehension about the place. What is it about old houses that frightens you, Kate Phenwick?"

"I don't think it's old houses themselves that frighten me," Kate responded. "It's just particular houses. There's something about Falmouth House, like Phenwick House, that seems mysterious to me. I confess I don't like to be alone in either of them. Yet I find myself from time to time with a desire to want to search about, as if I wanted to find something."

"Oh, precious Kate Phenwick," Rebecca said, putting her arm about her pretty daughter and holding the lilacs away, "there was something about you from infancy that was unusual. You were a happy baby. Still there were times when you appeared to be looking into the nebulous distance as if you could peer into the past. I had a feeling of extreme closeness to you from the start, as if in some other world we had been intimately involved. I doubt if I'm making any sense. I'm not the sort to speculate about romantic fantasy. I've never felt toward anyone else the way I feel toward you. I knew you from the very beginning—long before babies usually develop personalities. Perhaps that is why I only had one child."

As they went through the breezeway into the house,

Kate said, "I've always felt extremely close to you, too, Mother, in a strange way. I discussed such feelings with other girls, and few have had a similar reaction to either of their parents. They seem to have a distance that has never been between us."

Rebecca laughed softly as she went to find a vase in which to place the lilacs. "There has been a closeness, hasn't there? Many years ago I felt a similar nearness to my own father, the Reverend Elias Phenwick. He was always kind and loving to me. Then when I met my cousin, Johnny Ornby, I had another feeling. In both cases it was as if I had known them before."

"Before what, Mother?"

"That, Kate Phenwick, I don't know—except that your Aunt Jane once showed me a terrible portrait of a cousin. The girl had been deeply tormented, said to have been possessed by alien spirits," Rebecca related. "When I saw that likeness, I wept. I knew her, yet she had been dead for years before I was born."

"Rachel?" Kate questioned.

Rebecca looked astonished. "Why, how did you know that, Kate Phenwick? I didn't know about Rachel. Little has been said about her over the years. She was a family skeleton. Yet old Rosea Hackleby used to stare at me with a singular expression, folding her fingers together and sometimes cracking them. Once she asked me what the name Rachel meant to me. I replied, unhappiness. She asked me why. I told her I didn't know. As I was speaking an eerie picture came to my mind of a distraught young girl out by the old Indian camp—at least that's where I imagined it to be. She was talking to herself—or at least to unseen entities around her. Suddenly her body began to writhe in a tormented way akin to madness. I was confounded at even imagining such a thing. Rosea asked me what I was thinking, and I told her. The old lady just sat back and cracked her fingers again and said, 'Yes, I thought as much.' "

"What does that mean, Mother?"

"My darling Kate Phenwick, if I had the slightest idea," Rebecca replied, "I would tell you. I believe, after reading some of Rosea's books, that she put faith in something called reincarnation, that people live many lives and that they have a kind of attachment to other people and that they come back together—these people with problems or other situations they have to live out. You see, my father Elias was deeply in love with Rachel Phenwick as was my dear Johnny Ornby. That would not seem unusual except that she was a tormented child. After Papa fell in love with Rachel, he discovered he was her half brother, that Daniel Phenwick was his father, too."

"Danny?"

"That's what they called him, those who loved him," Rebecca said. "Poor tormented man that he became. His torment was from drink and dissipation, living the life of an adventurer . . ."

"And unhappy in love," Kate stated.

Rebecca shot her a startled glance before she nodded her head. "Yes, that could well be the case. I always felt sorry for Grandfather Danny. It was he who saved me when my life was in jeopardy. He saved me, but it killed him. He died for coming to my rescue."

"And Michael? Wasn't Michael with him at the end?" Kate asked enigmatically.

"Michael—Uncle Mike O'Plaggerty? Why, what made you mention him?" Now Rebecca was staring intently.

Kate shrugged. "Someone must have mentioned it."

Rebecca swallowed hard and tried to smile. "Uncle Mike was with Grandfather at the very end. He had cared for him in those last years. I have never seen such a devoted friendship between two men."

A sob caught in Kate's throat. She said nothing.

"I don't know what it's all about, Kate Phenwick," Rebecca sighed. "Perhaps we are related over and over again through a series of lives. I should hope we were. I should like to think that you and I would be together many other times."

"What about in Heaven?" Kate asked.

"In Heaven? If there is a Heaven, no doubt we will be there. I think that whatever comes after, that there is more after that, if you know what I mean."

"No, Mother, I don't."

"To be perfectly frank, I don't either, Kate Phenwick," Rebecca commented lightly. "You go out and gather some daffodils, we'll discuss this at another time. Will you go to Portland with Lydia?"

"If you think it best, Mother."

"I think it best that you—or at least one of us—visit Aunt Jane in her last days," Rebecca said.

Falmouth House in Portland rose like a phantom shadow as the carriage pulled up the hill overlooking Back Cove. The large, rambling, biggest house Augusta Phenwick had constructed stood with a marvelous view of the bay and the surrounding countryside, the lakes beyond. The trees had grown tall around the building, shadowing many windows, hiding the full facade from view of passersby outside the wall. Mystery rose like a mist around the old house. Time had aged it, giving it a permanent gray finish with black water streaks. The grass was a lush green and flowers bloomed everywhere, dispelling much of the gloom that emanated from the house.

Lydia Ornby, who had dreaded the coach ride from

Greenfield to Portland, had fortified herself with three different flasks of whiskey, which she inconspicuously hid and sedately imbibed of from time to time. She believed her actions had gone unnoticed. Kate understood her stepsister and her desire to drink as she did. Kate did not comprehend why, only knowing it to be a fact that she did. Only once did she broach the matter. Lydia had become irate in her reaction, denying she was excessive in the least.

Lydia indulged in gossip. Funnily enough, most of it she had heard at the saloon. Gossip about dirty little things whispered through the neighborhood intrigued her, the scandal, the suspicions. She lived vicariously through other people's adventure.

Upon arrival at Falmouth House, the carriage was greeted by the stableman and the guests by the butler. Lydia and Kate were ushered into the parlor.

No more did Kate enter the old building than that apprehensive fear came over her again. She wanted to run, to escape. What explanation could she give for her decision to do so? No, she must remain, put up with the edgy feeling and spend the required time visiting with the old lady.

"Can we see Aunt Jane now?" Lydia asked the housekeeper.

"She will be in the sitting room in a few minutes."

"Does she maneuver the stairs by herself?"

"Oh no. She has a room downstairs now. The first floor has been remodeled. The room behind the music chamber is hers. She doesn't climb stairs anymore," the housekeeper advised. "At ninety-five, she's lucky to move about at all, I should say."

"So should I," Lydia returned, a pleasant smile. Looking to Kate, she gave a blurry expression. "Why don't you look about, Kate Phenwick, and see if you find anything that attracts your attention?"

"I know this house upstairs and down," Kate commented without thinking.

"You do? I didn't realize you had been here that often."

"Well, I haven't been here since I was a child," Kate remarked. "But I do know the house. The music room is over there. The sitting room and the library beyond it. The dining room behind the parlor. Aunt Jane must have converted the room in which Rosea Hackleby stayed when she was a resident here."

"The room in which Rosea Hackleby stayed?" Lydia looked askance. "How do you all this?"

Kate smiled, blushing embarrassment. "I don't know. I guess Mother told me." She herself wondered. "I think I will have a look in the music room. Do you mind?"

"Of course not." Lydia was only too pleased for the girl to leave her in solitude.

The music room was neatly arranged. Eighteenth-century furnishings. If age had been allowed, it did not show. Everything appeared well kept and in order. Even the spinet was brightly polished, a fresh candle in the brass holder beside it. The shelves on the left wall as one entered contained several books. Pictures were about the room. A portrait of Jane as a young lady graced the wall above the spinet. A picture of Edward, Jane's brother; and one of Danny, her foster-brother. Kate stared at the likeness of Danny for a particularly long time. Again that feeling of uneasiness came over her that she had experienced upon seeing his image at Phenwick House. Then, as she turned to view Edward, a feeling of love and compassion seemed to move from her. He was someone to whom she had once been deeply attached, she thought. Her soft fingers reached up to touch the canvas as though she believed she could touch his face. She only touched the canvas.

Kate was distracted by a frightening portrait on the far wall. The small picture was that of a distraught young girl. How terrible! She noted it was not signed by Clayton Latshaw, but by a scribble she could not decipher. "Rachel," she thought, "poor possessed child." She wondered how she had known it was Rachel. Her mother had mentioned the portrait, it was obviously the same one.

The door to the room burst open. Plump, jovial Jane Augusta came bouncing in. She always entered a room like a breath of fresh air, radiant with smiles, a glistening pink expression, and usually perfumed with the scent of roses. "Ah, there you are, Kate," the woman exclaimed with a giggle. "Lydia said I might find you here. She seems to be enjoying her solitude in the parlor, nipping a bit—but we don't speak of that, do we?" Another giggle.

The two kissed.

"Cousin Jane Augusta, it's good to see you again after all this time."

"It's good to see you, Cousin Kate. I was just seeing to Grandmother. She's preparing herself. She wants to be as attractive as possible when she meets you. You mustn't be disturbed if she doesn't remember you. There are so many Ornbys and Phenwicks now, she doesn't keep them straight in her mind."

"Dear Jane was always the fastidious sort."

"I beg your pardon."

"That is, I remember Aunt Jane being proper and certain that everything was always in the right place," Kate fumbled.

"That's my grandmother," Jane Augusta commented. "I must admit I'm not as particular in the way I keep myself as she is. Still a splash of perfume and a clean, well-scrubbed face is enough to radiate one's personality as far as I'm concerned. Grandmother will be in in a few minutes."

"Sounds like my grandmother preparing herself for an entrance," Kate said with amusement.

"Well," Jane Augusta laughed, "I have to admit that my grandmother doesn't make the entrances that Aunt Patricia does. They're two different types of women."

"I know. Aunt Jane is quiet, subtle, while my grandmother is quite explosive, making entrances that no one forgets."

"My Cousin Paul is coming by in a little while," Jane Augusta announced. "I don't believe you've met him— Edward Paul Ornby. We call him Paul. He lost his wife two years ago this last spring. Being a widower has not agreed with him. A lonely man, I suspect, he comes often to see Grandmother. One of the few grandchildren who does. I suppose the rest of the family, like the Ornbys in Boston, don't have time for the old lady. I had hoped my brother Ted would come and examine Grandmother—he's a doctor, you know. Brother Daniel's a lawyer, you know."

"Daniel? Named for—" Kate hesitated.

"Named for Uncle Daniel, of course," Jane Augusta filled in. "I only recalled Uncle Daniel from when I was a small child. He was quite a handsome man even with gray hair and his infirm condition."

"He drank incessantly," Kate remarked.

"Well, he did at one time," Jane Augusta said uneasily, curiously watching her cousin.

"That's what I meant, *at one time*," Kate corrected herself.

"In his last years he was quite sober," Jane Augusta explained. "By then his body had deteriorated and his mind was a little—well, I shan't say weak, but distressed.

After all the man went through, such hardships, one could not blame him. Why, do you know, I was reading the account of when he was a small boy and he was kidnapped by some terrible person who actually threatened to cut off his hand if Great-grandmother Augusta would not pay a large sum of money to the culprit. It was absolutely horrifying! It's no wonder Uncle Daniel was as he was."

A picture of the basement at old Barrywell House flashed into Kate's mind. She saw a man who had only one hand and a hook at the end of his other arm. She felt threatened. Quickly she shook her head to erase that picture.

"Ta-ta, we won't speak of Uncle Daniel now," Jane Augusta said. "I can see that it distresses you."

"Why should it distress me?" Kate asked innocently.

"Well, I don't know that, Kate. I can't read your mind," Jane Augusta gushed. "It's the mental images that one conjures upon hearing such things."

A knock at the outside door.

"No doubt that's Cousin Paul now. I'm certain you will enjoy meeting him. He's a pleasant sort." Jane Augusta went to the music room door, pulling it open as the servant opened the large front door to the tall, slender man who had dark hair with gray streaks in it. His was a quiet handsomeness. His eyes sparkled and his smile was broad and friendly, especially when he recognized Jane Augusta.

"Dear Cousin Jane Augusta," Paul said, entering with his arms open. "Come give me a kiss."

Jane Augusta went to him, knowing that his expression was always demonstrative. He kissed her fully on the mouth as was his custom with all relatives. His glance went beyond Jane Augusta as he focused on Kate.

"Who is the lovely lady?"

"This is Cousin Kate Phenwick Cathcart, Rebecca's daughter," Jane Augusta introduced.

"I recall you were here years ago when you were just a little child. Now see how you've grown." Paul kissed Kate as he had kissed Jane Augusta. As he did a feeling of excitement went through the girl. She pulled her head back and stared into those vivid eyes, the smile that was invitingly friendly.

More than a little curious, Kate said, "Pleased to meet you, Cousin Paul."

"My pleasure." Paul turned to Jane Augusta. "I've returned this book. It's been beautifully printed, you're to be complimented, Jane Augusta. I like the title: *The Mysteries of Rosea Hackleby*. You've done an admirable job with it. Although I must say I don't indulge in such flights of fantasy or go along with all those eccentric theories the old girl has espoused. Still it is interesting. Have you seen this book, Cousin Kate?"

Kate shook her head.

"The real credit goes to Olivia Phenwick and a young writer friend of Aunt Patricia who edited it," Jane Augusta stated. "I merely kept the manuscript until it could get into the right hands. I brought a printed copy for Kate to take back to Phenwick House."

"I trust we will always keep a copy of it on our side of the family," Paul said, smoothing his fingers over the gold engraved cover. "Perhaps it will shed some light to generations to come—if anyone should be interested." He turned to Kate. "You really must investigate it, Cousin Kate. It's interesting if not factual reading. Old Rosea Hackleby wrote it mostly during her sojourn here at Falmouth House. For that reason alone it should remain in the family." He laughed, now staring intently at the pretty young girl he had just met.

Kate smiled. She felt awkward.

After a short initial visit with old Jane Ornby, who tired easily, Paul suggested that he and Kate leave her that she might rest. Jane objected, since she found the company pleasant. But she knew the danger of exhausting herself and the effort of preparing for the meeting had been tiring.

"You will join me for dinner this evening, won't you—my dear," Jane stated in a shaky voice. "What was your name again? You're Danny's grandchild, aren't you?"

"No, his great-granddaughter," Kate corrected. "Elias Phenwick was my grandfather."

"Oh yes, the child born—" Jane caught herself, "I was going to say not to Titter."

"Titter?" questioned Paul.

"Margaret O'Plaggerty," Kate replied. "She was Danny's wife—and—" she hesitated as the thought came to her—"and the sister of his best friend."

"Who was that, child?" asked Jane. "I don't recall."

Kate felt herself whiten, her hands begin to tremble. "Why, one of the O'Plaggerty boys—Michael." Why the funny sensation that came over her? Realizing that all eyes were on her, she added, "The O'Plaggertys—at least their descendants—still live in Greenfield. Patsy O'Plaggerty is a good friend of mine."

"Michael?" Jane said softly. "Yes, dear Mike. He was a sweet boy. He was very close to both Edward and Danny. I believe he was always envious of the fact that Mother adopted Edward and me—we were Munsks then—and not him. Mike loved Edward and Danny as if he were their brother. I had completely forgotten about Michael. Oh my, what time does to a person's memory."

"We won't detain you any longer, Grandmother,"

Paul stated, rising and going toward the chair in which Kate was seated. "I would like to take Cousin Kate for a little stroll about the grounds, perhaps down to the hill and along the waterfront of Back Cove . . . if she'll go with me."

Kate was flustered. The conversation had disturbed her. Paul's attention was even more disquieting. "A stroll? That would be pleasant." She wanted to escape the interior of that house for a while. Paul had come to her rescue.

Paul walked with his hands stuffed in his pockets, breathing deeply of the fresh, warm air. "Grandmother's a dear. But it's sad to see her slowly losing her faculties. She will no doubt ask you your name a hundred times during your visit. Sometimes she even forgets who I am. She speaks a lot of the past. I suppose that is natural, those were happier days."

"Dear Jane always had a way of holding the family together," Kate commented, "when they began to scatter. She was always the kindly mother hen, while Grandmother Patricia was the matriarch."

"Dear Jane? That's twice you've used that expression," Paul observed. "It seems unusual coming from a great-grandniece."

"Does it? I didn't realize I was using it. I meant to say Aunt Jane," Kate returned. "I wonder what I could have been thinking. My mother says I have a curious way of referring to people."

"It sounded as if you've studied up on the Phenwick family history," Paul commented a few minutes later as they neared the shore of Back Cove.

"Living at Phenwick House—" She stopped. What was she going to say? "I mean, Mother has told me tales of the family."

"I should have liked to have known Uncle Edward and Uncle Danny. Grandmother does speak of them quite often," Paul remarked. "She was very fond of both of her brothers."

"And they were no doubt fond of her," she said. "How could they help but be, as sweet as she is?"

Another period of silence passed as they walked near the water's edge. Kate viewed the scenery. It was all so very familiar to her, yet it had changed. To her right were three large, ancient gravestones. There was no other evidence of a cemetery. She stared at them curiously as she slowed to a halt.

"Now what has captured your attention, my pretty one?" Paul asked, following her gaze. "Gravestones?"

Slowly Kate approached them. The names that had once been prominent upon them were eroded away. Only one date could be read: 1763. She reached her hand to feel the numbers.

"Do you know there's a secret entrance to an underground tunnel behind this stone?"

"An underground tunnel?" Paul laughed.

"It leads to the basement of Falmouth House," Kate explained. Then she quickly added, "My mother told me about it." (Rebecca had not, but it was the only way she could justify her statement.)

"Your mother must have known Falmouth House well."

"I suppose she did." How did she know about that entrance? Or was it just her imagination? "There's a lever back here," she said, reaching to the side of the stone. "You pull it and the stone can be pulled back. It's not really a grave after all. The other two are real tombs, though."

"Can you pull the lever?"

"It's stuck."

Paul reached around and touched it. "There's a lever all right. I'll have to take your word that it releases the stone . . . or at least that it used to." He caught her hand. "You're a curious child, do you know that?"

"My father used to call me Kate, the curious," she said with false laughter.

"A strange expression for a father to use," Paul returned.

"Maybe I'm a strange person, Cousin Paul." She looked down at their hands still wrapped about each other. Excitement was moving through her.

"And you're beautiful and lovable—and I'm going to kiss you again. Will you mind?"

"I think not," Kate whispered. "I rather hoped that you might."

"A cousinly kiss?" he asked.

"If that is what you prefer."

"No, Kate, I would prefer another kind," Paul replied.

Her eyes glistened with excitement as his face came closer to hers. In a moment their lips were touching. He was a man well experienced in that. She tingled until she felt herself pushing away from him. Her reaction was alarming. Despite his nearness, his touch, she was distracted between kisses long enough to glance again at the gravestone. Then her attention was back with the man and the realization that she must not too greatly encourage his passion.

# CHAPTER SIX

John Tyler Collier traveled extensively with Clarence Hoskins for nearly a year. The young man managed to work odd jobs, while Hoskins hustled about in whichever town they chanced to be, proclaiming that he was a detective and that was the only line of work for which he was suited. Often he went his own way for several weeks at a time, but he always returned to look up the industrious young man. John was strong and capable of doing a good day's work. During that time he devoured whatever books he could get, memorizing long passages and self-educating himself in the finer things of life.

From Quincy, Illinois, the men went downriver to Hannibal, where they spent the remainder of the summer. Hoskins got an assignment to trail a man to St. Joseph and asked John to wait in Hannibal until he returned. John obtained a job sweeping out a general store and running errands. He was soon permitted to wait on some of the customers, but the store owner, a suspicious sort at best, did not trust the young man to handle money. That feeling of lack of confidence from his employer caused John to get itchy feet and it was all he could do to force himself to remain until Clarence returned.

By autumn they had moved on to St. Louis. John helped a farmer with his harvest, working for room and board. Then, as the cold weather began to set in, he found a position stoking the furnace on a riverboat that ran between St. Louis and New Orleans. His intention was to go as far as New Orleans and quit. But Hoskins, who was able to get an assignment that took him to Kansas City, persuaded the young man to sign on for the return trip to St. Louis and come back again. By then Hoskins should be back in New Orleans.

John put in long hours on the riverboat. He kept very much to himself. Over and over he read the notes he had translated from Clarence's scribbles on the day he was allegedly hypnotized by Homer Dillsworth. He memorized all the names and facts given, wondering what the puzzle was really all about. What little free time he had, he spent in thought, many hours leaning at the rail, staring dreamily into the muddy Mississippi. Going toward winter, the water journey was more comfortable, the terrible humidity less oppressive.

The boat's captain said he had been observing John and believed that, if he cared to, he could get a better job as a deckhand instead of being a stoker, which was really work for a black man anyway. John considered the move up in position until he realized that that would have too much of a feeling of permanency, and he had already decided that someday he would go to New England, to Boston, to look up the Phenwick family.

The next time he landed in New Orleans, John informed the captain that he would not be returning, even as deckhand, on the riverboat. He had saved a little money, enough to live for a month or so in New Orleans if he was careful. Much of the menial work was handled by the Negroes in that extreme southern area. Being from Illinois, he was considered a Northerner. While he never voiced his opinions about abolition, it was naturally assumed that he was in favor of freeing the slaves.

Hoskins showed up again in New Orleans, relating wild tales about the adventures that were going on out west. The gold rush in California excited the detective and he yearned for an opportunity to go in that direction. John could not be persuaded, since his dream was to go northeast, no matter what promise of wealth lay west.

John took work with an elderly man, who taught the youth how to keep his books. John was not experienced in mathematics, but his employer was patient with him. He learned quickly and within a month was able to handle the books with no problem whatsoever. Pleased with his accomplishment, John decided that he was suited to an office position and one which required mental ability and skill. His penmanship had improved and his talent with figures emerged outstandingly.

By March of 1854, when Hoskins announced that he was taking a position that would involve him for several months, he begged John to go along with him. After all, he expected to be in San Francisco by summer.

John declined the offer and bid his friend farewell. Besides he had gotten as far as he had on his own and he was dubious about the positive effect that Hoskins or a trip to California would have on him. During those months he lived in a small room in the rear of his employer's house. He had become almost obsessed with desire for education.

One spring day while John was strolling through the Vieux Carré section of New Orleans, he became fascinated by a sign in the window of a shop advertising the art of a card and palm reader. A large drawing of a hand with all the lines marked on it and surrounded by playing cards captured his attention. As he stared at it, he became aware of two dark eyes staring at him.

The woman was in her forties, plumpish and seductively slouchy, he thought. Her olive-colored skin and Negroid features indicated to him that she was a person of mixed races. Not unusual in New Orleans. Her head was wrapped with a red scarf that was too expensive-looking to be considered an ordinary bandanna. Golden earrings in large loops hung at the side of her face.

"You want Carmen to read for you?" she asked.

"Who's Carmen?" he asked awkwardly. "I mean, I can read pretty good for myself."

"De cards?"

"You mean playing cards?"

"And Tarot cards," the woman said. "Twenty-five cents and Carmen will tell you de whole future of your life."

He sneezed and look around to see if a flower vendor was in the vicinity. Wiping his nose with a large handkerchief, he smiled awkwardly at the woman.

"Fifty cents Carmen read de cards and de palm," she persisted.

"A tree? Oh, you mean my hand."

"*Oui*, I mean your hand." She reached to take it. John held back, not certain he wanted this person of dubious-appearing character to touch him. "Do you have fifty cents?"

John fumbled in his pocket, feeling coins. "Well, yes,

I do. But I don't know I want to waste it on any tom-foolery."

"It won't be wasted. Carmen give you de good advice. Carmen see de past, de present and de future," she urged.

"The past?" John questioned, weakening.

Carmen still had hold of his hand and had positioned it so that she could see the palm. "Ah! Oh! I see dere is much love in your life." She stared up at the man. "Only fifty cents, mistah."

"Love?"

"You come in, Carmen read for you." She practically pulled the reluctant young man into the building.

The place smelled musty but heavy with incense. A small table with a chair on either side of it was in the center of the small room. A deck of worn cards and an imperfectly shaped crystal ball was on the table. Two small candles burned at the side.

"I will burn de violet incense . . . just for you."

"No," John responded. "Violets make me sneeze, if it's all the same, ma'am . . . I mean Miss Carmen."

"Den I burn frankincense and musk," Carmen said. "Dey will bring up de spirits from de past to hover around you to give Carmen de messages about you."

John watched as she lit the incense from the candles, then turned and motioned for him to take a seat at the table.

"You put de fifty cents on de table before Carmen start. I no take before I finished," she smiled as she spoke, "but I be sure you have de money."

John fished out the coins and placed them on the table.

"You shuffle de cards and make a wish," Carmen instructed. "Tink only of you wish."

John shuffled the cards and wished he were in Massachusetts. After he had cut the cards in several piles as instructed, Carmen gathered them and began slapping cards onto the table.

"Ah, I was right about de love I see in you hand. You gonna be married and have fine children," Carmen droned. "I feel cold weather around you. Snow. Ah, and here is you wish card right here. You have much big love. I tink you know who dis woman is, but you no have meet her. Do you know what I mean?"

"No."

"You know her from past," Carmen said cryptically, "not from dis life. You two love many times before but she was not always a woman just as you not always a man in past lives. I see you travel, go on big boat to where snow fall heavy in wintertime."

"To my home in Illinois?"

"No. Far away dan dat," Carmen said. "Let me look at you hand again." She took it. "Ah, *oui*, much travel on boat—ocean travel. Will be soon. See dere, dat line, I tell you about love and children. Carmen no wrong. You must work hard for another year, maybe two, den you have much money."

"How will I have much money?"

"You marry lady what has much money. She pretty, too."

John was beginning to get excited. "When do you see me leaving New Orleans? Before summer, I hope."

"You go to big boat company," Carmen said, "and get job going on ocean. Job waiting for you now. Carmen see much happiness for you. You have any questions?"

John stared at the palm of his hand for several minutes. "Yes, there are two names that stick out in my mind. Can you tell me about them?"

"What is names?"

"Michael . . . and Danny."

Carmen scattered the cards face down and instructed

him to pull seven of them. She closed her eyes as he picked the cards. Slowly, pensively she turned the cards over one by one.

"Good friends ... in past life ... Now Danny not a man dis time ... spirit come back as woman. Dat good. Now love between Michael and Danny can be different kind. Before it was friendship, now will be husband and wife—very much in love. It is so beautiful as Carmen see."

"Was *I* that Michael that you see?" John asked, coming all over prickly with excitement. "Is that what you see?" He sneezed. "I thought you were gonna burn frankincense and somethin' else." He wiped his nose.

"I did."

"I smell violets." He sneezed again.

Carmen laughed gaily. "Violets is in you mind." She wiggled with excitement, too. "Oh, I see why. One day dey no more make you sneeze, den you be happy. Dat all I can tell you."

"You didn't answer my question. Am I that Michael?"

"You already know de answer to dat, *mon ami.* Now if you have another fifty cents—" She winked.

"No. I have no more money with me," John said, rising excitedly. He shook the woman's hand. "Thank you very much. Goodbye."

Before Carmen could speak, John was out of the building and running down the street, leaping occasionally to kick his heels in the air.

The next afternoon John called at the offices of a shipping company. The man in charge looked at him, reaching to feel his biceps and generally sizing him up. He offered him a job as a deckhand on a ship traveling between New Orleans, Le Havre, France, and Savannah,

Georgia. John was to report two days later with his belongings.

John had studied enough maps to know that Savannah, while still in the South, was on the east coast. A jump in the right direction, he thought. He left a note for Clarence Hoskins with his old employer and prepared for the voyage that would take him closer to his ultimate destiny.

# CHAPTER SEVEN

Edward Paul Ornby was forty-six, twenty-seven years older than Kate Phenwick Cathcart. During Kate's visit with her Great-aunt Jane, Paul was a regular caller, not so much to see his grandmother as he was to see Kate. The girl was overwhelmed by his charm, his poise, his maturity. Never had she known an older man toward whom she had developed romantic notions. The only mature man she really knew was Osgood Wymer and he had never asserted himself in a masculine way.

Paul would always greet Kate with a kiss, as he greeted both Lydia and Jane Augusta. Even Jane Augusta noted that her cousin was kissing her other cousin in a different way. Was Kate actually encouraging the man? Lydia observed, too, but she was not the romantic that Jane Augusta was.

"Kate, may I have a word with you?" Jane Augusta

asked early one afternoon when the girl was ready and waiting for Paul to come pick her up to go for a ride.

"Yes, what is it, Cousin Jane Augusta?" the girl returned, uncertain how to read the expression in the other's face. "Is something perplexing you?"

"Come into the parlor where it is cool," Jane Augusta invited. "Life at Falmouth House is slow-moving, isn't it? Sometimes I feel as if I'm just waiting for death to arrive."

"Yours, Cousin Jane Augusta?"

"No, don't be silly, girl," Jane Augusta scolded. "For Aunt Jane I meant. She is getting weaker and weaker. I do wish my brother Ted would come and have a look at her. It isn't natural for people to live to be so old. Poor Aunt Jane is in terrible pain. Life is an effort for her."

"Must you stay?" Kate questioned.

"I would only have to make a return trip when it's over," Jane Augusta commented with a sigh. "I'm Aunt Jane's youngest son's eldest child. I have more or less taken over the responsibility of taking care of such matters on the Ornby side of the family. Aunt Jane used to do so."

"Is that what you wished to speak to me about?" Kate asked.

"No, Kate, it isn't," Jane Augusta said, setting her face in a determined expression. "My concern is for you."

"For me?"

"I've observed you with my cousin, or should I say our Cousin Paul. He is a dear sweet man and I wouldn't say anything malicious to hurt him in any way."

"What are you getting at, Cousin Jane Augusta?"

"I think you know, Kate," the woman stated, trying to force a congenial smile and at the same time maintain a stern expression. "I am not unobservant. I have witnessed the byplay between you and Cousin Paul. I can see where such could inevitably be leading. You should know that Cousin Paul has been married. He's a widower and has three children; all of whom are older than you. He married young. The fact is, although I know it is often a tendency of Phenwick women to marry older men, I cannot help but believe that the years between you are extremely vast. I don't see how you can have a common interest."

"What is this about marriage, Cousin Jane Augusta?" Kate questioned, straightening her back and raising an eyebrow. "I have no intentions of marrying anyone at the moment."

"Then are you indulging in immoral behavior with Cousin Paul?"

"Of course not, Cousin Jane Augusta. I should think you would know better than that," Kate exclaimed angrily. "Furthermore I think you should know your Cousin Paul better than that. He is a fine gentleman and treats me with great respect."

"This fine gentleman with whom you are going riding this afternoon," Jane Augusta stated, "while he was married to his wife, even when the children were young, was known to be a philanderer and to consort with women of low moral character. Fact is, he was discovered in the embrace of one such woman by his father-in-law. Had it not been for Aunt Jane, it would have created a tremendous scandal in Portland. I believe Aunt Jane made a financial arrangement which was pleasing and satisfying to the injured father-in-law."

"That was when Cousin Paul was very young, I suppose, if it is true," Kate said.

"It *is* true. Confront him with the matter," Jane Augusta suggested, "and while you're asking, mention several other episodes he has had with ladies of singular repute. I can think of at least a half a dozen. And those are only the ones of which I am aware."

"Why are you telling me this?" Kate inquired, fear mixed with anger rising within her.

Jane Augusta rose and went to the girl. "Oh, my dear Kate Phenwick, don't you understand? I want to protect you, to save you from a reputation that could be disastrous to you. You're still so very young and Cousin Paul is extremely experienced. It seems an innocent, passing lark at the moment. As time goes on, his approach will alter, becoming more and more persuasive. I have no doubt he has developed a technique that is most convincing and effective on an innocent lady like yourself."

"Jane Augusta, I don't want to hear any more of this," Jane scolded. "I am really very fond of Cousin Paul. I don't think you should say such disparaging things against him. Even if you're not making them up, I don't want to hear them."

"Don't you understand, I'm telling you this for your own good. I don't want to see you hurt."

"What can I do? Simply tell Cousin Paul I can no longer see him or go riding or strolling? Never to have dinner together again in a quiet little restaurant?"

"You may do whatever you please, Kate Phenwick, but I know there is a good chance that you can do irreparable damage to your heart. It is so wise to save one's love and affection for a man who truly loves you."

"Where am I going to meet such a man?" Kate asked. "I think I am somewhat in love with Cousin Paul ... *now*. He has never once been ungentlemanly toward me."

"I have noticed how he kisses you, Kate, when he enters the house. It is not the polite cousinly kiss he gives to Lydia or me. Rather there is implication of romance in his approach to you, and insinuation. If you do not realize that, Kate Phenwick, you are more naïve than I thought you were."

"But he is good and kind. I have only the fondest affection for him."

"Because he has persuaded you to have it. He has presented himself in a pretty light," Jane Augusta commented. "But beware, my dear. As I say, I love Cousin Paul dearly—but I wouldn't trust him beyond the next few minutes."

"Knowing Cousin Paul has made my stay at Falmouth more endurable, less oppressive than I thought it might be," Kate said, now beginning to fidget when she spoke. "I confess I like his attention. For that matter, I enjoy his kisses."

"They excite you?"

"Very much so."

"Then that is leaving yourself wide open for attack," Jane Augusta stated. "And from attack, heartbreak. At the present time, I have recently discovered, you are not the only young woman Cousin Paul is seeing. There are several others."

"I can't believe that," Kate responded, staring coldly at the woman. "How can you say such a thing?"

"The truth is often difficult to confront, especially when it involves someone with whom you have a romantic interest," Jane Augusta said.

"I feel you're being malicious and gossipy," Kate declared in a raised voice.

"No such thing, my dear. I'm not even being presumptuous, other than to mention this to you now. I have investigated the rumors about Cousin Paul, looked into the stories about his past and discovered that he has led a considerably jaded life. It is said that his late wife long ago became aware of his adventures and indiscriminate habits. She never broached the matter to him, but held her thoughts deeply within herself until they gnawed at her insides and ultimately destroyed her. She did her best to keep such information from their children, but they have learned of the truth, they know about their father. They try to overlook it." She chuckled. "Children have a way of doing that because they love a parent. My brother Ted, who is a doctor, spoke with Cousin Paul's late wife, Louise. She confided in him her hurts and fears, most of all her desire for death, to escape living with a man she had come to detest, whose closeness she could hardly abide, yet who was her husband. I don't know it for a fact, but Ted suggested that she tried to take her life at one time. Perhaps that is what brought about her final termination. Once a person has developed a habit pattern such as Cousin Paul's, and it is allowed to endure over a substantial period of time, that habit is difficult if not impossible to break. That person continues in the practice of it, regardless of what circumstance comes into his life. Oh, dearest Kate Phenwick, how can I make you understand what I am trying to say?"

"I believe I understand you quite well, Cousin Jane Augusta," Kate replied. "That being the circumstance, if you will excuse me, I will go to my room and prepare myself for a nap. When Cousin Paul arrives tell him that I'm indisposed, not feeling well, if you will." With that she rose and walked stiffly from the room.

Certain that Jane Augusta would follow her part of the way, Kate hurriedly went around the hallway to the dining room and the kitchen beyond. She needed something to calm her nerves. A glass of milk perhaps. Her stomach was churning. She was not too certain that milk would sit well. Perhaps only a glass of water. Anything to help her swallow her pride.

Near the door to the kitchen, there was another door

which led to the basement. Kate stopped and stared at the basement door as if she expected someone to emerge from it. Curiously she put her hand to the knob, twisted it and pulled it open. The stairway was dark, yet light fell into it from the hallway. Beside the banister was a container of candles and matches for the benefit of those who ventured into the cavern below.

Kate lit a candle as though something magnetic were attracting her to that place. Slowly she took the stairs, making certain she was steady on each step before she took the next. Fortunately she was not wearing a wide skirt, but one that could be maneuvered through such a narrow passage.

The first room to her left attracted her attention. She went to the door. Before pushing it open, she said to herself, "This is the laboratory." Upon entering, she found there was a large table in the center of the room and a workbench. Indeed, it could have been a laboratory of sorts. The room was relatively clean. The cupboards were filled with jars of preserves. It was now a storage pantry. A basket of potatoes was at one side and the last of the previous year's apples. A strange feeling came over her as she stood in that mysterious room. What had she encountered? Why was the room vaguely familiar to her?

A lantern was on the table. Discovering it had oil, she put the candle to it and turned up the wick, causing more light to be cast about. Why did the name of Rosea Hackleby come to her?

For a few moments she considered the recent conversation she had had with Jane Augusta. She knew the woman was basically well-meaning and the essence of kindness. Still she did not want to believe those things about Paul. In that stillness she realized how deeply her feelings were for the man and that he could easily have gotten what he desired from her for the asking. A picture of Ronald Boggs flashed into her mind. Were all men the same? She wanted to cry, but tears would not come.

She left that room with the intention of going back upstairs. Instead she turned to her left and penetrated a long, solemn corridor. Dirt floors. The walls, while supported by timbers and rocks, were covered with heavy coats of dried and hardened mud. The deeper she went into the tunnel, the more fearful she became. The tiny lantern light was barely enough to dispel darkness on all sides of her. She could hardly see her way. Yet she recalled the gravestones she had seen on her first walk with Cousin Paul. Recalling that she had said one of the stones was the secret entrance to the basement of Falmouth House, she realized the corridor must eventually lead to it. How did she know about that gravestone? Or that the tunnel led to it? It was all a complete mystery to her.

"Kate Phenwick! Kate Phenwick!" Jane Augusta's voice called from somewhere above. "Kate Phenwick, are you in the basement?"

Her first impulse was to hide the lantern and pretend she was not there. She pushed against the wall, putting the light on the far side of her.

"Kate Phenwick! If you're down there, please come, it's very important," Jane Augusta called.

Apprehensively Kate stood in silence.

"Kate Phenwick!" Jane hollered again. "It's Aunt Jane! I've sent for the doctor. She's desperately ill and is calling for you. If you're down there, please come if you wish to see her alive again."

That pronouncement startled Kate. She hurriedly made her way back through the tunnel. "Yes, Cousin Jane Augusta, I'm coming. I'll be there in a few moments."

As Kate moved through the passageway, she had the sensation that she had done so many times before. That caused an eerie sensation to permeate her entire being.

# CHAPTER EIGHT

Jane Ornby's voice was feeble, but her words were clear. Kate approached the old lady's room with Jane Augusta. The door was slightly ajar. Surely Aunt Jane must have overheard when Jane Augusta called her in the basement, warning that Kate must come if she wished to see the old woman alive. Kate felt herself flushed with fear, hesitant to go to the room where death was approaching.

"You are not ever to molest any of your relatives, Edward Paul," Jane was saying with measured words, her voice shaky. "I am displeased with you. I had but hope in your future. But you have disappointed me these past years. The stories I've heard of your indiscretions are notorious. Now your cousin. Surely you're not such a fool that you could mistreat her."

"I've not mistreated her, Grandmother," the distinct voice of Paul Ornby replied. Kate could not see him from where she was standing. There was no doubt in her mind who was speaking.

"Not yet, Edward Paul," Jane said, "but you were on the brink. I know your habit pattern. It's been the same story over and over again. I would think you would have had the common decency not to attempt such a liaison among your own kin."

"Kate is a distant relative."

"I don't care how far removed she is, she is still my late brother's granddaughter. Your reputation with women has been scandalous. I'll not have you misleading this poor girl. Do you understand?"

"You've made yourself very clear, Grandmother," Paul returned. "I promise I will not proceed with my intentions."

"See that you don't. I have made provision in my will that, if you cause another heartbreak of any kind, I will disinherit you and insist that you be a family outcast from that time on. Is that perfectly understood?"

"Yes, Grandmother, do not harp on it, please."

"Do you have any idea how much time I have left? I don't. I would hardly call that harping—not yet," she said with a slight chuckle.

Jane Augusta rapped at the door before sticking her head through the opening. She asked permission to enter.

"Yes, by all means. I've quite finished with Edward Paul," Jane replied.

Jane Augusta held the door for Kate to enter. She stood in the archway, not certain she wanted to go farther. Staring at the pathetically withered old lady, a feeling of repulsion came over her. Jane was gently propped up in bed, her skin nearly as white as the bedding. Kate had never seen the old lady in such a state of illness. Jane had always prepared herself and put on a youthful attitude. Now she seemed a helpless bit of flesh and bones with a tired heart. Her hands were like claws, all bones and skin. The rings had been removed because they rattled with her slightest movement. Her mouth seemed sunken and her eyes hollow.

The old woman attempted to smile, her eyes brightened. "Well, well, I didn't expect you yet, Danny, but I'm awfully glad you came. Come closer, won't you?"

Kate looked to Jane Augusta, who motioned her into the room. The girl wanted to correct the old lady, instead she silently stepped to the foot of the bed and held onto the knob on the bedstead.

"Oh, I was mistaken," Jane said. "In this strange light I thought you were someone else, my dear. Who is it? Susannah? Rebecca? I know the face, don't I? But I find it difficult to place the name."

"I'm Kate Phenwick," the girl replied.

"Oh yes, my dear, how silly of me to have forgotten. You must realize that my old mind is not what it used to be, it plays games with me. My eyes focus on one thing, but seem to see something else. For a minute I thought you were my brother. Of course, that's foolish. Danny has been gone these many years. Still there was an aura about you, the way the light fell on your face. I see it's you. Won't you come and kiss me? Or is it repulsive to you to consider showing affection to a withered old lady."

Kate went and kissed her aunt on the cheek. She touched Jane's hands, which were motionless, which could not even find the strength to reach up.

"I'm pleased you came to be with me, Kate Phenwick. You're a very pretty girl. Mother would be pleased with you. Perhaps she already is. Did you ever smell the violets?"

"The violets?" Kate asked.

"Yes, Mother comes with the scent of violets. It was one of her favorite aromas. So often in the spring I would gather little bouquets of the lavender flowers—so fragrantly sweet—and put them in teacups on my mother's table. When I say my mother, I mean Augusta Phenwick, of course. My own mother, Lydia Munsk, is just a faint memory. Augusta was always the mother I seemed to love the most. Perhaps because I was closer to her all those years. You've been exploring Falmouth House, haven't you? I should think you would. There is much for you to see, many memories that I have, memories of the past, of my brothers. Not only the Phenwicks, but my dear brother Uriah Munsk. He was the rebel, the different one, the only one in the entire lot who opposed Edward and me being adopted into the Phenwick family. Yet of all of them, he was perhaps more a Phenwick than any of the rest of us. And dear Edward ... I long to see him again. We were so close. I wonder ... yes, I wonder if I will."

Kate moved back to the bedpost, clinging to it, her fingers moving restlessly.

"I have a feeling about Danny," Jane said, attempting a broad pleasant smile. "Isn't it funny how we have feelings? Rosea used to say they were premonitions, intuitions, that we should listen to them, heed what they have to say ... for it is in a sense the universe speaking to us. Rosea had a quaint way of putting things. I loved her. With all her eccentricities and wonderful old devices, she was a sweet woman, very knowledgeable and ahead of her time. One day her books will be priceless."

Paul exchanged a quick glance with Kate. His look was that of a small boy who had been severely reprimanded. He went to the bed, kissed his grandmother on the cheek. "Grandmother, I'm going to take a little walk now, if you don't mind. I think I need the fresh air."

"You *do* remember what I told you, don't you, Edward Paul?"

"Yes, Grandmother, and I will abide by your wishes, although I don't think you understand me or realize how I will be affected by your ultimatum."

"I don't believe it important that I understand you, Edward Paul," the old lady replied. "I know of your past. Just bide my words. Unlike my mother, I don't particularly wish to remain ghostlike among my family. Perhaps I will, perhaps I won't. It is unimportant. I'm looking forward to whatever is there. Augusta ... perhaps Edward. I don't believe Danny will be there."

Paul kissed his grandmother again, clasped her hand and slipped from the room, only gliding a contrite gaze past Kate.

"What was I saying, my dear?" The old lady made a faint sound of laughter. "It is unimportant. All that is important to you now is to find happiness and contentment. If you can do that, you will have pleased me. Now I think it time for the doctor, Jane Augusta," she said, feeling a slight pain, yet intuitively desiring to be alone. "The others needn't come. If they couldn't come to visit while I was alive, what point is there appearing to view the remains? Ta-ta. Jane Augusta, this young lady seems as if she could use a cup of tea. Is that not so, Kate Phenwick?"

"Yes, Aunt Jane, I think I could use a cup of tea." The girl went to kiss the old cheek lightly. Before tears could come to her eyes, she turned quickly and practically ran from the room.

Jane Augusta lingered only a few minutes, kissing her grandmother and valiantly holding back her own tears.

"I will go prepare the tea now. I'm certain the doctor is on his way. It will only be a matter of moments."

"A matter of moments? As I look back, that seems to have been all that life was—only a matter of moments. Don't weep for me, Jane Augusta. You have always been a good granddaughter. Although we have not spent that many hours together, I have always held a special place for you. Now you will truly be the head of the Ornbys. Not a Phenwick woman, alas. But I wonder if having such a title is all that important in the final analysis. I suppose to some it is. I've enjoyed the reputation." She sighed. "Now leave me in peace. Have the servants usher the doctor in when he arrives."


Jane Augusta prepared the tea herself, putting the leaves loosely in the teapot and letting them steep for precisely the time she believed necessary. She carried it on a silver tray into the parlor where Kate was seated, a handkerchief in her hand, doing her best to control tears. Occasionally she dabbed at her eyes, which had become red. She made a brave attempt at smiling, at presenting a pleasant although forced expression.

"The doctor's arrived. I saw him pass the door with a servant while I was sitting here," Kate informed. "He's with Aunt Jane now."

"She'll be all right. It's those of us left living that have the real problems." Jane Augusta set the tea things on the table and offered little cakes with the cup and saucer. "I like my tea a little strong. I always say what's the point of having it if you don't have the taste of tea. Otherwise it is merely hot water, don't you think, Kate?"

"Yes." Kate looked abstract, glancing from her cousin toward the window and the gentle summer scene outside.

"I'm sorry you had to overhear Aunt Jane reprimanding Paul. He's really incorrigible. I know you wouldn't take it from me, but perhaps Aunt Jane bolstered what I had to say."

"What I don't understand is why I must have so many disappointing experiences with men," Kate commented.

"So many? You sound like a worldly woman, Kate Phenwick," her cousin responded with a giggle.

"No, I'm not. There was Ronald Boggs and now Cousin Paul. It seems like so many," Kate remarked. "When one so desperately wants to be in love—and for as long as I can remember that has been the driving motivation of my life, to experience love. Perhaps that was because I loved my father so very much."

"Daughters have a way of loving their fathers. He is a male image, a masculine figure. Sometimes I used to think of Eustace, my late husband. I would compare him with Daddy. They weren't the same at all. Eustace was quite different, somewhat slovenly in his appearance, while Daddy, like all the Phenwick men, was proud. He had a marvelous carriage and a beautiful disposition for a lawyer. A man of character and determination. Eustace on the other hand was not useless, but certainly he lacked the drive my father possessed. I believe I loved him very much. I loved Eustace, too, in his way. No, I don't miss not being in love, or having a man. I've grown used to living by myself over the years. Eustace died so early in our marriage. I think of him every so often, and imagine that his spirit is lingering about me. That is enough for me as far as love and that sort of thing go. I'm not calloused, Kate, but I've had the experience. Let me put it that way and leave it at that. You were saying."

Kate sipped from her teacup. "Only that for as long as I can remember love has been a strong motif in my thinking. I wonder why that is? Patsy O'Plaggerty, one of my best friends, says it is because I developed toward womanhood earlier than other girls. From earliest recollections, I thought of love. It's as if I had been born with love on my mind, that that was my whole reason for living this life. Do you understand what I mean, Jane Augusta?"

"Not precisely, my dear. What *do* you mean?" The plump lady blinked.

Kate laughed awkwardly. "It's difficult to explain. I've often had the feeling—while I was walking along the seashore for instance—that I was not alone, that love was walking with me—whatever love is. Many times I felt the sun kiss me, the wind caress me, the ocean engulf me in passion ... not erotic, but very sensual, understanding. It's as if I was meant to love deeply in this life. I just get that feeling. Then when Ronald Bogg came along and he seemed so attentive, I aimed that love motif toward him. I guess I idolized him in a sense, he was the personification of love. I was disillusioned. He was a mortal ... only a mortal, and I was searching for a god. He fell from his pedestal when he attempted to become physical with me. As I resisted, I knew that mirror of illusion was being shattered. I could see him for what he was: an untamed animal with no more concern for me than a stud stallion has for a mare. That is what hurt me when I had been carrying such an idyllic dream."

"Oh, you poor child, to have experienced such a thing," Jane Augusta sympathized.

"No, no, not a poor child at all. I was fortunate, for it gave me perspective," Kate replied. "Yet when the situation arose again wherein I came in contact with another man, who seemed to be the personification of love—I'm speaking of Cousin Paul, of course—I lost my perspective. I admit I was like a piece of clay in his hands. But I didn't want my god to become another mere mortal. When you were speaking today and as I overheard Aunt

Jane, I knew that is what Cousin Paul was. Will all men be that way to me?"

"No, my dear. Your godlike individual will appear, I have no doubt. You have clung to a dream. True, in the search you have had unfortunate encounters, but that too is part of learning. Have you finished with your tea?"

"One cup is sufficient, thank you."

"I want to read your tea leaves."

"Can you do that?"

"Rosea Hackleby taught me years ago when I was just a young girl. It's a very simple process. Put the saucer on the cup and turn it over. As you hold to the teacup, make a wish."

Kate did as she was told and handed the cup and saucer to Jane Augusta.

Jane Augusta studied the design of tea leaves on the side of the cup and those fallen onto the saucer. "Oh my, would you look here! There's a perfectly shaped heart. That can only mean love, my dear ... beautiful love. Here's a young man. He almost looks like a statue of a Greek god. I saw three pictures once of statues. I see happiness, great contentment. Not far away either, very close." She examined the tea leaves on the saucer. "Oh yes, mountains of love. And here—children ... three ... four ... There may be four, but if there are one will not live very long. It will distress you a little since you will consider all your offspring love children. Why shouldn't you? You have so much happiness and love here."

Kate laughed. "Jane Augusta, I would like to believe you. I would love to think that was all going to come true."

"Believe in it, Kate. Believe that you will have an idyllic love. For, as I see it, you will. It is just practically

95

around the corner. You see this sharp angle? It's going to come out of the blue. When it does, well, you'll think you've found your soul mate. I wouldn't be surprised if he isn't your soul mate."

"My soul mate?"

"I do hope so. Then your love will be truly idyllic."

# CHAPTER NINE

As with every crisis of her life, Lydia Ornby took the death of Jane Phenwick Ornby as a traumatic episode which was her own personal tragedy. As a result she had begun drinking long before the old lady passed over into that other level of vibration and continued to do so for the next several days. She would begin early in the morning by having a few drinks in her room. Then she would attack the brandy bottle in the library, or the sherry decanter in the music room, and proceed from there. She usually managed to leave the house about noon, parasol in hand, to sashay down the hill into a nearby business district where there was a saloon which she could enter. Most such taverns did not permit ladies. That particular one was of low estate, hence allowed anyone to enter.

Most of the habitués of that saloon were lost individuals; the women were usually creatures who had had unhappy love affairs or had abandoned hope of fulfilling any sort of romantic dream. Many were persons of loose morals, whose principal desire in life was to become stupefied with intoxication.

Lydia personally knew none of those persons, nor did she permit any sort of verbal familiarity before she was well on the way to inebriation. Then she began to relax somewhat. While she maintained an arrogant exterior, she was actually crying out inside for someone, anyone to become her friend. Generally that friend presented himself in the form of a man. Unless he was a hopeless imbiber, his thoughts verged on the prurient.

While not adverse to expressing herself physically, Lydia was not motivated by such, or at least she presumed she was not. If a man's approach was too forceful or obvious, she would rebuff him; or would coyly flirt with him, keeping him at arm's distance while he purchased her enough drink to break down her resistance.

Unfortunately during that time, whenever she had more than a few drinks, Lydia burst into tears, lamenting her poor dead Aunt Jane. She had not had any particular closeness to that relative, but she had visited her from time to time simply out of boredom and a desire to escape Greenfield.

Three days prior to Jane Ornby's death when the diagnosis indicated no other outcome, word had been sent to Boston, apprising the family that the oldest living Phenwick woman was on her deathbed. Since Jane Augusta sent the message, she made it sound imperative that a representative group of the family were expected in Portland.

When Patricia Phenwick received word, she instantly gave the information to Marcia. The younger Phenwick woman was expected to make whatever arrangements were necessary. Patricia could not make the journey, as Marcia well knew. As the principal Phenwick woman of Edward House now that Patricia had relinquished that position, Marcia was the obvious one to inform the rest of the family. She suggested that she would go as Patricia's representative. She hoped her dearest friend, Nancy, and her husband Peter could make the journey as well.

By that time Marcia had discovered that she was very much in love with Stuart Phenwick. Although she had been sociable with other young men of Boston, none offered the personality or the pleasant good looks of Stuart.

Augustus Phenwick had passed over two years before. Peter, his father, had stepped down as head of Medallion Enterprises in Boston, leaving Peter's grandson, Stuart, as top man in that organization. Hence, Stuart was away at that time, traveling to Savannah to check with his Uncle Prentise on the interstate operations of the shipping company. He also wished to sample the climate of the antagonism of the South for the North and the effect it would have on business.

Marcia had never made an ocean trip with Stuart. Each time he was away, her longing for him became greater. When he returned she could hardly let him out of her sight—a sure indication that the pretty young lady was deeply in love with the man and her days of flirtation and playing the game of choosing were over.

Peter and Nancy agreed to make the journey, preferring to go by rail from Boston to Portland, which by then was well established and the quickest means of travel. That decided upon, Marcia packed a few belongings and made final arrangements for the three to make the trip.

Now an ordained minister and more pious than he had ever been in a fundamentalist way, Gordon Phenwick saw his relatives off at the railway station. He sent his condolences and assured them that he would pray that dear Aunt Jane had a place in Heaven.

Marcia could hardly wait to get away from Gordon's overbearing fanaticism. The more he had preached fundamentalism, the more she had turned against it, embracing what was referred to as the New Thought movement, espoused by men like Emerson and other philosophers in and around the Boston area. She could not believe in a traditional concept of Heaven and Hell. She made her beliefs known emphatically to Gordon, the only one of the family who openly took him on as an opponent. Nancy Phenwick always sided with Marcia, convinced of the metaphysical approach to philosophy.

Kate experienced strange emotions as a result of Jane Ornby's death. Not only was it the physical fact that the old lady no longer occupied the withered shell of flesh; she felt she had a strong tie to Aunt Jane. She thought it significant that the old woman had mistaken her for Danny. Why did she ever-increasingly think of that man who had been her great-grandfather? She had heard more negative things about his character and his life than she had heard positive. Yet she could not help but feel a certain alliance with his memory, and perhaps his spirit—if it were hovering about.

Kate was also troubled over the emotional reaction she had had to Paul, and the fact that she believed she had been in love with him. The feeling was gone, he had been unmasked. Beyond anything else, she felt deceived and brutally used by the man.

She had fallen into a state of depression, which caused her to feel listless and unmotivated. She caught herself drifting about as if looking for something to catch her attention. Finding that she could only do so much exploring of Falmouth House, Kate spent time thumbing through many of the books from the library shelves. On other occasions she found herself engrossed in the writings of Rosea Hackleby. She sensed the mysteries recorded therein could well have a particular meaning to her. Time and again she read the passages dealing with reincarnation and the old woman's belief in the continuation of life as the soul moved from one plane of existence to another, returning again and again to the physical body to learn specific lessons required of it.

At times she had the definite sensation that images that were presenting themselves to her mind must be memories from the past. Were that the case, there would be an explanation why things she seemingly saw for the first time were familiar to her. She dared not speculate too long on such topics because they left her with a confused attitude, a bewildered state of mind.

When Peter Phenwick arrived at Portland with his wife Nancy and his Cousin Marcia, he went immediately to see that all the arrangements had been taken care of for the old lady. He discovered that Jane Augusta had efficiently seen to the details.

The body was laid out in the parlor of Falmouth House. The relatives spent many hours in the vicinity, as if holding a wake. They were waiting for other family members to arrive.

Kate found difficulty entering the parlor. The sight of the discarded debris in the casket bothered her. The first glimpse was enough. The body had served its purpose and was no longer of any earthly use as far as she was concerned. Aunt Jane was no longer there. The morbid thought of spending hours with the lifeless remains left Kate cold. The periodic outbursts of the drunken Lydia were disquieting.

On the day before the formal services, Kate had left

her assigned room on the second floor. She had taken the back stairway, desiring to go outside for a breath of fresh air. The warm morning attracted her. As she reached the first floor of Falmouth House, she observed the door leading to the basement. What strange impulse came over her, magnetically drawing her to the entranceway? Hesitating without, a strange compulsion came over her. Why must she go below again? What was down there that seemed to have a haunting hold on her?

Beside the door she found the container of candles. Lighting one, she carried it to the basement and the room to her left which had once been the laboratory of Rosea Hackleby, wherein she had written a large part of her book of occult mysteries. Finding the lantern she had previously used, she lit it to examine the room. What a vast maze of chambers were in the subterranean area of the house.

She left the erstwhile laboratory and raised the lantern wick as high as it would go. She plunged forward into the hallway, again going to her left, instinctively knowing there were only pantry rooms to her right. How did she know that? She would not permit herself to dwell on that thought. Holding the lantern high, she searched into the room next to the one in which she had been, to discover it was a place where the laundry was done. It was cool and comfortable in the summer. The floor was laid with stones. Washtubs hung on the wall. A large working area was in the center of the room. There were a fireplace and a stove where the servants heated water and the irons with which they pressed the clothing.

Leaving the laundry room, Kate penetrated the corridor, which was stone-paved part of the way. Upon examining the room on her right as well as the one directly across from it, she discovered them to be for storage, filled with old furniture, children's toys, dolls, relics from childhood's past. The next room down to her right was filled with other neatly arranged objects. The smell of mildew was poignant. Closing the door quickly, she went across the hall to the room on her left. Hesitating, she became aware of a strange vibration that seemed to move beneath her feet. She held the lantern low to examine the ground—only a dark spot, a stain. Had it been made by blood? If so it had been there for many years and had become a part of the floor.

The door to the room was poorly hinged, causing it to scrape into the dirt when she pushed it inward. Upon entering, she discovered an old bed, hardly more than a wooden pallet, a rickety table and two chairs that had seen far better days. A singular sensation passed over her as she stood in that room, a familiar impression flashed to her mind. A haunting aura of mystery hung heavily. She knew that bed, she had been on it. She had sat at that table. Before she raised the light to see, she was certain a niche was in the wall to her right which had probably been meant to be a closet. As she had previously observed, the basement walls were thick and were covered with hardened earth.

A sound whined through the basement corridor. Fear mounted within her. Could it have only been the wind whispering through? Or had someone walked past the door? She closed it as best she could. Again the sound of movement. A soft moaning followed. Like a child caught at something he should not be doing, she went to the closet niche and pushed herself against the wall. The door handle seemed slowly to turn.

Putting her hand to her mouth, tremors of fear plunging through her, she was certain at any moment she would be accosted. Why should she fear any living soul in the house? The thought calmed her momentarily until she analyzed what she had perceived. The word "living" might have been the wrong choice. Was she being haunted by some ghostly presence that long had trod the basement corridor? Perhaps a mysterious earthbound spirit that could not leave the place of death.

Kate's next impulse was to extinguish the lantern. Aware that she was without matches, she turned the wick down as low as she could, hoping the tiny flame would not be detected. Yet she realized that the passerby must surely have become aware of the flickering lantern. Her presence was obviously known. Setting the lantern on the floor, she pushed against the wall. The earth from which the walls were made dirtied her dress. She couldn't care less about her appearance in that desperate moment. As she pushed her back tightly to the wall, something jabbed her shoulder. Sharp-pointed. Repositioning herself, she used her hand to discover that it was actually angular, as if it were part of an oblong container sticking from the wall.

After some minutes of waiting in terrible anticipation, but not being intruded upon, Kate raised the lantern wick and examined the projection from the wall. The corner of a metal box. Back in the room she found a blunt piece of metal which looked as if it had once been a knife, now rusted and misshapen. Taking it with her into the niche, she used it to gouge around the object of her curiosity.

After several minutes of digging, dirt beneath her nails, and feeling grimy, she managed to unearth the container, which was about eighteen inches long, ten inches wide and eight inches high. It was extremely heavy. She perceived the metal to be lead.

She carried the container to the table, which creaked beneath the weight of it. Diligently she worked at opening the box. The blunt instrument came in handy as a lever to force the lock and pry the cask open. She was astonished to discover a cache of old coins and jewels—a fortune, she thought. Instantly into her mind flashed a picture of Ben Strothart, the alleged pirate, who had initially created the Phenwick fortune. Was this part of his booty, his ancient treasure? The thought amazed her. Instinctively she knew Augusta Phenwick had buried that casket in the wall. How could she be certain of that? She was mystified. Clayton Latshaw's name came to her mind as she recalled his dignified signature at the corner of several paintings. Why had she thought of him? Was it because she had heard someplace that Clayton Latshaw had designed Augusta's houses? Perhaps it was his ingenious idea to hide the treasure where it was.

Kate closed the lid after only lightly brushing her hand over the jewels, touching one or two of the gold coins. A queasy sensation squirmed in her midsection and she felt as if she were going to be sick. Had some mysterious vapor risen from the treasure chest?

Finding the steadier of the two chairs and putting the lantern on the table beside the casket, she sat facing the bed. Something happened in her mind. Her vision became hazy.

Suddenly she was aware of the figure of a man sitting on the wooden pallet, a drunken expression on his face. Was she somehow glancing into the past? Did she actually see an image before her? Although the door did not open, a young girl came into the room, whom she judged to be no more than fourteen or fifteen years of age. The girl had a distraught expression. Kate was certain she recognized her from the portrait of Rachel Phenwick—the one reputed to have been possessed by alien spirits.

Kate was aware of no dialogue as the girl entered. The man, with graying hair and several days' growth of beard, looked up with dazed vision and recognized the girl. He held his arms open to her. Instinctively Kate realized she was indeed witnessing a scene from the past that had occurred in the room as though she had somehow penetrated the barriers of time and was able to receive the vibrations that once had happened there.

Suddenly the girl was attempting to become familiar with the man, who fought her away. The girl viciously scratched at him. The madness that had possessed her was almost overpowering. As Kate watched that struggle, it slowly faded. There was no longer an image at all. Terrified, she ran from the room, taking only the lantern with her. Running along the corridor as fast as she could, she climbed the stairs without stopping for breath.

When she reached the first floor of Falmouth House, Kate ran directly to the parlor as if some ghostly apparition were chasing her. Bursting into the parlor, she startled the mourning members of the family. Her distraught expression of terror and shock mobilized the family to move to her. Marcia was the first to reach Kate, putting her arms about her and trying to console her.

"What is it, Kate?" Marcia asked. "Are you all right? What has happened?"

"I just saw something horrifying."

"Something horrifying?" Peter asked, reaching to touch the girl with a comforting gesture.

Nancy said, "I d'clare, she's as white as a ghost."

"Or as white as if I'd seen a ghost," Kate exclaimed. Almost incoherently she tried to explain what she had experienced.

Kate was offered a glass of brandy which she declined. Questions were fired at her from all sides. Jane Augusta patted her hand. Nancy was duly concerned.

"I swan, Mistah Phenwick," Nancy remarked, "I do believe you and perhaps one of the menservants should go down and investigate what's going on down in the basement."

"You're right," Peter acknowledged. "I think, it would be well if Kate were to accompany me."

"Shall I go with you?" Marcia asked.

"No. It would be best if Kate and I went alone. Will you be able to accompany me, Kate?"

Kate looked at the still handsome, but aging, gray-haired Peter Phenwick. He was similar in appearance to the ghostlike man she had seen in that dreadful room. "Yes, Cousin Peter. With you along with me, I would have less fear."

Marcia and Nancy walked with the two as far as the entrance to the basement. Peter insisted they remain behind.

Carrying the lantern, Kate showed Peter the exact room where she had discovered the treasure.

"I confess I didn't know my grandmother very well," Peter said. "The great Augusta Phenwick was an enigma to me. I was still a boy when she died. She was friendly enough, as I recall. I admired her, yet I could not tolerate what she had done to my mother. For that reason I was not very close to the woman."

"She died at Phenwick House in Greenfield, didn't she?" Kate asked.

"Yes."

"Your father died there, too, didn't he?"

"Yes. Your mother was being pursued by a villainous black man. My father went to her rescue. He was no power against a much younger and stronger man. He died a short while later while being attended by Uncle Michael."

"*Uncle Mike?*" Kate questioned. "Are you speaking of Michael O'Plaggerty?"

"Yes. He was not really my uncle. At one time he was Elias' adopted father until we realized that Elias was actually our half brother. We always considered Uncle Mike close. As children, Lex, Elias and I—even Rachel—were far closer to Uncle Mike when he returned from his travels than we had even been to my father. Uncle Mike was filled with love, and we knew it. Children sense that sort of thing. I haven't thought of him in years. He was a very good man, and very devoted to my father."

"I think the image I saw was that of your father—Danny. And I suspect the girl was Rachel," Kate whispered.

"Perceiving vibrations from the past is something I know nothing about. I was never all that friendly with Rosea Hackleby," Peter said. "I didn't go in for her gibberish about the occult and the mysteries that occur. No doubt she would have a theory and, to her, a logical explanation about what you witnessed, if indeed you actually saw something happening on the bed."

"If I didn't see it on the wooden pallet, where did I see it?" Kate questioned.

"Where else, dear Kate, but in your mind?" the old man said.

"In my mind?"

"Imagination."

"Why should I imagine such a horrible thing? That girl was trying to physically molest her father. She was doing—well, I can't tell you what she was doing because it was that shocking."

"I understand that such an incident happened between Rachel and my father. I don't know the details. It was related to me by another person—I don't recall who. I know as the ultimate result of Rachel's death and that of my mother, that my father refused to drink again. He was a changed man. I thought the things he told me that happened in those years were imaginary. He compulsively drank himself into a stupor at regular intervals. I believed those things were hallucinations, the imaginings of a drunken mind."

Kate thought Peter was insinuating she herself had been hallucinating. "If you think I—"

"I didn't mean to imply that you were under any sort of influence when you were down here," Peter commented. "I merely meant to tell you of the circumstances of my father." He moved from the girl. "As to the treasure, it is no doubt one of the many Grandmother Augusta had hidden. It belongs to you, Kate. You found it. That is part of the legacy, the treasure goes to the finger, no matter who it may be. I don't wonder that these old walls haven't been torn down by the servants or others who have been searching for Augusta's treasure. It seems, if I may be philosophical, that the treasures appear only at the right time, and to the person to whom they are meant to belong. I will carry it upstairs for you and assure the rest of the family that it is yours."

As Kate stood staring from her cousin to the wooden pallet on which she had witnessed that frightening phenomenon, again it seemed as if the ghostly vibrations appeared. She watched as the man fought off his daughter's advances. This time she heard words:

"How was I to know as a child, Papa? I had feelings I had to suppress, needs that never were fulfilled." She reached to his chest and gently stroked it, her movement progressively becoming more intimate. *"I had need of thy love."*

"But don't you understand, I was never capable of

loving," the old man confessed, "not your mother or you."

"*Lovest thou not my brothers?*"

"Oh yes, they were boys, not fragile and different," he explained, becoming aware of her caressing movement. "Yet I couldn't deal completely—Rachie, what are you doing?"

"*What thinkest thou I'm doing?*" Her hands became more clawlike and her features changed from the pretty face of a young girl.

"My God! What's happening to you?"

"*Thou shalt give me thy love this night to make up for all the years thou hast kept it from me,*" she said, her voice crackling and caustic. Now her talons were searching over a larger area of his person.

"Rachel! My God! You're supposed to be up on the second floor in bed!"

"*Tied in bed, thou meaneth.*" She pulled him to her and forced a kiss onto his mouth.

The man spat. "You smell of foul odors!"

Her hands were exploring all over him and he was fighting to resist her advances. As he did, she started clawing, digging deeply into his flesh until he was crying out with pain. Uncanny strength filled the girl's body as she began ripping the clothing off him, tearing flesh with the cloth, and while she tore at him, she attempted to kiss him again and again.

"You don't understand about me," the man managed to say as he was being overpowered. "No! Oh, God, no!"

"*Calleth not on Him, for He heareth not thy pleas,*" she managed to say between grunts and groans. "*He hath forsaken thee. Only Master Beelzebub canst help thee now! Surrendereth to me and thou shalt be his for-*

*ever.*" Her mouth covered his and it was putrid and offensive. "*Shrinketh not from me!*"

The man gagged and shortly after vomited.

"No! No! I can't stand it anymore!" Kate screamed. "Make it go away, Cousin Peter!"

"Make it go away? Make *what* go away? There's nothing happening in the direction you're staring," Peter returned, going to her and shaking her. "You are seeing things I cannot see. There is no reality to it—nothing there but an empty bed."

She screamed. He slapped her face.

"An empty bed?" As she shook her head from the momentary stunning slap, she saw there was indeed nothing on the wooden pallet. "Oh, my Lord! What's happening to me, Cousin Peter? Why? Why have I seen this?"

Peter hugged her to him. "Poor, poor Kate. What vicious memories are coming to you from the past? I must get you back upstairs. I no longer have great strength. We will leave the treasure here and send one of the trusted servants back to get it. Come along, Kate. I only pray that you are not as tormented as poor Rachel."

"Do you think me going mad, Cousin Peter?"

The understanding man caressed her. "No. Not at all. I believe you have come to this house and somehow tuned into the past. Tell me one thing. Did you have the sensation that you were one of those two people you were watching?"

Kate was still whimpering, terrified with shock. "I don't know what you're saying, Cousin Peter."

"Were you one of those persons?"

Kate thought a moment. "I don't know." She suddenly had a picture of herself being held in her mother's arms. Rebecca was warm and loving to her. "Take me upstairs.

I want to leave this place and return to Greenfield as quickly as possible. I want my mother."

"Your mother?" Peter did not voice what he was thinking. Instead he helped the girl from the room, through the corridor and up the stairs where Marcia and Nancy took her and led her into a quiet room where she could relax.

# CHAPTER TEN

The first ship that John Tyler Collier signed on traveled from New Orleans to Le Havre, France, stopping in several ports along the way. The young man worked hard, doing the tasks of two men. He was devoted to his job, every day pressing harder and harder to accomplish whatever he could, taking on increasingly more responsibility. During those days at sea as he felt he was becoming a qualified merchant seaman, winning the respect of captain and crew, he kept a daily journal of his thoughts and ambitions. While in the English port of Liverpool, he picked up several books to augment his collection that he had taken with him from New Orleans. His leisure time was occupied with study. Daily he increased his knowledge. Largely keeping to himself, John associated with few of the crew members in a fraternizing way, although he worked side by side with them diligently helping where others would stand back and watch.

The return voyage took him to the city of Savannah, Georgia. The ship was to return to New Orleans. By then John had so thoroughly learned geography that he realized New Orleans would be going the opposite direction from his ultimate destination. He informed the annoyed captain that he would not be continuing to Louisiana. Instead he would try to find a ship going north, hopefully as far as New York.

Arriving in Savannah, he discovered an uneasy atmosphere. The hot climate created a certain lazy attitude. There was trouble in the air, anxiety among the people. More and more he overheard talk about secession of the southern states from those in the North. The anti-abolitionists were angered. Often he listened to the speeches of irate Southerners who upheld their rights to maintain Negro slaves. John had never been sympathetic toward slave owners, believing all men were created equal. Negroes were persons just as he was. He knew better than to engage in public arguments over such issues.

John Collier was not a drinking man, although he occasionally had a glass of beer with fellow seamen. His limit was one, from which he rarely devoured more than a few sips. Occasionally he smoked a corncob pipe; even that he did in extreme moderation.

John had spent three weeks in Savannah unable to find a place on a ship going north. Few companies were traveling from south to north, the commerce was decreasing between the two areas of the country as tension over the slave issue was growing.

Bill Simmons was still bartender at the Seagull Tavern on the wharf. The beefy man had put on weight over the years and loomed as a threat to any of the rough sailors who sought to perpetrate a fight in his establishment. Basically he was a sociable sort who enjoyed speaking with the seamen, discussing their problems, their fantasies, their love lives, the things men who went to sea talked about. Also, he was aware of what was happening in the shipping industry concerning hiring and availability of positions aboard the vessels.

When John Collier entered the Seagull Tavern late that particular afternoon, more to get out of the oppressive heat outside than to take libation, he went to the counter where Bill Simmons was working.

"What'll it be?" Bill asked. "I d'clare, it's hotter'n blazes out there, ain't it?"

"Yes, it is. Just give me a beer," John said, putting a coin on the bar.

Bill served him. "What's th' problem, lad? I swear ya look like ya've done lost your last friend."

"No. I don't have a last friend—not really," John returned with a faint chuckle. "The only old friend I've had in years parted company with me back in New Orleans when he went out west."

"Ya a seaman?"

"Of sorts. I just came back on the *Marybelle*. It returned to Louisiana. I want to go north."

"Ain't too many companies ship north these days," Bill said. "Medallion still goes there, that's 'cause they got their main office in Boston. Hard line t' get onto. Then there's th' Preston Line. They still tote cotton an' t'bacca up to New York. I'd reckon if'n ya wanted t' go that way, it'ud be best t' see if'n ya could git a job on one-a th' Preston ships. I understand they's a-lookin' for men on th' *Atlantic Queen*. They've problems, ya know. Men come down from th' North—those who sympathize with the South—an' stay. Ya kin't blame 'em none, they're Southerners at heart."

"The Preston Line, you say?"

"You ain't a Southerner, are ya?" Bill asked.

"No sir, I'm from up in Illinois, around Quincy."

"Wal, I don't right know where that is. Is it north or south?"

"It's not a slave state. It's mostly farms—practically on the Mississippi River," John explained. "I'm a farm boy. Guess that shows, doesn't it?"

"Not t' me, it don't. Ya sound like a real educated man t' me," Bill allowed.

"My mother taught me to read and write and do a few figures," John said, "but I've learned a lot on my own. I got a whole bag full of books I carry to sea with me. Seems like I got some kind of quest of knowledge."

"They why ya waste your time a-goin' t' sea?" Bill questioned.

"That's where I have time to study," John replied. "The Preston Line, you say?"

"Yeah, th' *Atlantic Queen* was hirin' on this mornin'."

John left the Seagull and went directly to the Preston office. Before long, he had signed aboard the *Atlantic Queen*, which would be departing Savannah the following day.

Later that afternoon, John strolled over the wharves looking at the other ships in the harbor. The sea held a strange fascination for him and he had an avid interest in ships. He did not have extensive ideas about making a career of sailing, but he had always been the type of person who took an active concern in whatever job he was doing.

As he neared the pier at which the *Mercury*, a Medallion ship, was docked, he went forward to watch as the cargo was being hoisted aboard. The black slaves were shirtless and glistening with perspiration in the afternoon sun. The man in charge was pushing the men.

A carriage had driven out onto the pier. A tall handsome man alighted from it and observed the workers as he paced about examining the cargo. Fancily dressed, he looked out of place on the docks.

A load of cotton bales was being raised. John's eyes followed it as the load rose high into the air. Suddenly he became aware that one of the bales was not securely held in place. It began teetering and slipping out of position. The tall well-dressed man was standing directly beneath it, concerned with remote activity at another spot. The hoisting rope jerked, the bale fell.

Reacting with remarkable precision, John ran forward, grabbed the handsome gentleman about the waist and practically lifted him from his feet and carried him far enough away that they were both clear of the exact spot on which the cotton bale landed with a bounce. An instant later, considering the distance the object had dropped, John realized it would have struck the gentleman with a shattering force, severely harming him, if not taking his life.

"Good God!" the man exclaimed.

John released his hold around the man and pointed back at the fallen bale. "That just missed hitting you, sir. Forgive me for the physical contact, but I knew of no other way of saving you."

Several men had gathered around the excitement.

The tall man caught his breath, dusted his clothing and managed a broad, personable smile at John. "I'm certainly grateful to you, friend." He looked up. "I can see I came very close to losing my life. What can I do to repay you?" He reached into his pocket for his wallet.

John motioned for him to put it back. "Please, sir, I don't want no money for that. I just didn't want to see you get hurt."

"But I must give you something."

"You already have: a friendly smile and a word of thanks," John returned. "Besides, I believe that I might need someone to help me someday and a good deed will come back to me. That's what my mother always said."

"Well, that's awfully good of you, my man, but I feel I should give you more than that."

"Forget about it, sir," John said. "Return a good deed to somebody else when he needs it."

Another well-dressed man was hurrying down the gangplank of the *Mercury*. A moment later he arrived at the man who nearly got hit.

"Good heavens, Stuart, I just heard you almost had an accident!"

"I came very close to it," Stuart replied. "But I'm all right, Uncle Prentise. This man—well—where did he go? I'll be switched. One of the seamen managed to grab me out of the way before the bale hit me."

"Get in the carriage, Stuart Phenwick," Prentise ordered. "I'm taking you out to the house, where we can relax and visit with Harriet and the children. It's dangerous hanging around on those piers when they're loading. You might have been killed."

Stuart craned his neck to see if he could spot the man who had come to his rescue. "I've never met a person quite like that seaman. He wouldn't take any money. That was the least I could give him. You don't find that attitude with too many people." He laughed curiously. "I wonder if he actually existed, or if he was some sort of guardian angel come down from Heaven to save my life."

"I doubt you'll find many angels on these wharves, Nephew," Prentise said, his square jaw braced as he held his eyes to scan the milling men. "Come along now."

"If I ever run into that fellow again, by God, I'm going to do something for him," Stuart stated. The handsome Phenwick heir was obviously deeply impressed by that act of heroism, and he would not forget it for years to come.

While John Collier had had a few adventurous episodes in his life, especially when in the company of Clarence Hoskins, he thought of himself as a basically good person. Such was a reflection of the good moral sense his mother had instilled in all of her children. Kindness radiated from him, which was often mistaken for naïveté. His mind was open, exploring, wanting to learn. His appreciation of beauty and his gentle manner made him prey to bullies. He quickly displayed he was no weakling if there ever was any doubt about his manhood. Always he maintained an attitude of fairness, and he avoided physical violence whenever possible. Yet he would never walk away from a matter of honor or principle. Perhaps that is why he was often a loner, staying to himself, building dreams and ideals toward which he could strive.

Although he had memorized the notes Clarence Hoskins took when Homer Dillsworth accidentally had put him under hypnosis, John would read and reread the copy he had made. He wondered if he would one day discover the mysterious Phenwicks and the soul mate that was allegedly his among them.

Such thoughts pervaded his mind in the days to follow as the *Atlantic Queen* tossed and glided over the ocean. When he was not busily at work, or studying, he would stand at the rail in some secluded place on deck and stare off toward the horizon, or down at the splashing water.

"Mine if'n I join yer?" a coarse voice asked as a burly seaman came up beside him at the rail one evening. It was one of John's few acquaintances aboard the *Atlantic Queen*, Delbert Longneck. The man had a beard and usually wore a knit cap to cover his bald head.

"Come ahead, mate," John answered. "There's plenty of room."

"You're always at dreamin', ain't yer?" Delbert remarked after studying the lad for some time.

"Dreaming ... thinking ... memorizing," John responded.

"Yer keep pretty much to yerself, I notice," Delbert said. "Some sailors're like that." He poked him lightly. "Guess you're dreamin' 'bout th' girls, ain't yer?"

"Not all the time." John laughed.

"Me, I am. But they kin be a handful, mosta 'em," Delbert alleged. "I notice yer ain't like most seamen. Why, I just got winda somethin' 'bout yer that really surprised me."

"What's that?"

"Ol' Billins was tellin' me 'bout yer on the dock in Savannah," Delbert continued, "an' how yer saved that fancy feller's life. Billins said he'da been a goner fer sure if'n yer hadn't tackled him."

"I didn't realize Billings had seen that," John commented. "It was nothing. A man's in trouble—I try to help out. It didn't cost me anything."

"Oh yeah?" Delbert laughed mockingly. "Billins said th' dude offered yer a reward an' yer never took it."

"Why should I? If you helped me avoid some kind of danger, would you expect a reward?"

Delbert scratched his head and tugged at his beard. "Well, reckon I wouldn't, seein' you're a mate, but that feller was rich. Yer know who that man was?"

"No, nor do I much care," John replied.

"He was one-a th' owners-a Medallion, that's who he was."

"Medallion?"

"Why, if'n yer had played her cards right, yer coulda got yerself a good position aboard one-a their ships," Delbert commented. "Maybe made one-a th' officers. Yer got th' makin's fer that anyway."

"I didn't know who he was. Besides, it wouldn't have made any difference. I wouldn't have used something like that to get a position."

"Why not? Better men than yer have," Longneck said. "Why, yer was practically belly t' belly with one-a *the* Phenwicks, that's who he was."

"The Phenwicks?"

"Th' Phenwicks-a Boston, that's who."

"Oh, I never—are you certain?" John asked. "*The* Phenwicks?"

Delbert Longneck laughed. "Now where's your righteous attitude, Johnny?" He swatted him on the shoulder and walked away.

Had John actually been that close to the Phenwicks? But would he have acted differently if he had known? The questions bounced around in his brain. He would remember that man's face. Still he had no idea that the Phenwicks owned Medallion Enterprises. Maybe it was not even the same family. Then again, maybe it was.

# CHAPTER ELEVEN

Jane Augusta returned to Greenfield with Kate while the other Phenwicks went back to Boston. Kate had been so distressed and upset over the incident in the basement at Falmouth House that she could not stand the idea of being alone during the trip. Lydia had decided to stay in Portland where she could enjoy city life—a vast contrast to country living. Besides, she had met a man, a saloon habitué, who had taken a drunken fancy to her, and she to him. Lydia had inherited her father's share of Jane Ornby's fortune and she was not about to return to the mundane existence she had known in Greenfield.

"Do you want to talk about it, Kate?" Jane Augusta asked as the carriage bounced over the uneven road.

"What is there to speak of, Cousin Jane Augusta? It seems madness runs in the family," Kate said. "Maybe I'm afflicted with it, too."

"Nonsense, child! What a thing to say!" Jane Augusta exclaimed. "Why, you're as sane as the rest of us. What makes you think madness runs in the family?"

"Look at poor Rachel. When I saw that picture of her in the music room at Aunt Jane's, it nearly made me ill," Kate expressed. "She must have lived a terribly tormented life."

"Rachel wasn't insane, not really. According to Rosea Hackleby she was possessed by two alien spirits of old witches, women who had been tried and executed during the witch trials in Salem. They had taken over her body. Why, Rosea said that whenever one or the other would get control they spoke the very same way that they do in the Bible. You know, *thees* and *thous*, *speaketh* and *goeth*. She said she knew that that was no more Rachel speaking than it was the man in the moon. And the sound of the voice was different. I asked old Uncle Uriah Munsk about it, and he, too, said there was no doubt in his mind that Rachel was possessed by some unearthly forces. They would argue right there inside of her body. It's all written down somewhere. Probably in Rosea's book."

"*Thees* and *thous?*" Kate asked, remembering the hallucination (for what else could it have been?) she had had in the basement of Falmouth House. Peter had been with her, but he had been oblivious to what she was actually experiencing.

Jane Augusta went on, ignoring what Kate had just questioned. "I can't remember the exact place it is in the book, but we'll look it up."

"I have heard stories," Kate said a few minutes later, "that Rachel's mother was mad."

"Rachel's mother? That would have been Aunt Margaret. Margaret O'Plaggerty she was before she married," Jane Augusta informed her. "Rosea told me about her, too. She was married to your grandfather—Uncle Danny. It was a kind of strange marriage. Great-grandmother Augusta had been fond of Margaret, who was the daughter of faithful servants who had been with her for years—in those days they were called slaves. Augusta had them indentured to her." She giggled mischievously. "I guess there was a reason Augusta liked Tim O'Plaggerty. Well, that's neither here nor there. The fact of the matter is, Margaret was the daughter of a slave and therefore hardly material from which Augusta thought Phenwick women should be made. She turned on the girl when she discovered that Danny was going to marry her. I think he decided to do that out of spite anyway. Augusta tormented Margaret on this side and the other side of the grave—actually haunted her, they say. Then Great-uncle Danny would stay away from home for long periods of time. Some say he liked Margaret's brother, Michael, better than he liked his wife. I don't mean to imply anything by that—it was a perfectly wonderful and innocent friendship, I have no doubt. Where was I?"

"Michael O'Plaggerty?" Kate asked mysteriously. "*Michael?*" What warm feeling had come over her?

"Michael, like one or two of his brothers, remained a bachelor all his life," Jane Augusta informed. "Rosea was always very fond of Michael. He was one of those people everyone liked. Rachel was especially fond of him—and so was Margaret. He tried to help them both. I suppose you know that your grandfather, Elias, was not a legitimate Phenwick at birth. Oh, there was no doubt he was Danny's son and had his good looks. He was born to one of the Mumford women, who raised Elias, letting him grow up with his own half brothers Lex and Peter—and with Rachel. Well, when the Mumford woman got cantankerous and attempted a little extortion,

Michael stepped in and adopted Elias. There was a monetary arrangement. So in a sense Michael O'Plaggerty was your foster-grandfather—at least until Elias chose to be a Phenwick. It's so very confusing."

*"Michael?"* Kate questioned again as if she had not heard Jane Augusta's chatter about the family. "I feel I should know Michael O'Plaggerty. He must have been an uncle to my friend, Patsy."

"No doubt he was if Patsy's an O'Plaggerty," Jane remarked. "I only met him once. I know I was very impressed with him."

Kate wore a distant smile. "Would you know him if you were to see him again?"

"Land, child," Jane Augusta exclaimed, "Michael died a year or so after Uncle Danny. He just sat down in a chair one day and died."

Kate became remote, turned her head away from Jane Augusta and watched the passing scenery. Her thoughts were confused, but a kind of contentment seemed to fill her.

"I don't want to hear anymore, Kate Phenwick," her mother stated emphatically after the girl described her uncanny experience in the basement at Falmouth House. "I'm sorry, dear, but the pictures that come to my mind are too vivid. I don't want to hear of such things. I've heard enough about Rachel Phenwick to last the rest of my life. She was a poor unfortunate person and that's it."

Rebecca Phenwick never told anyone, much less her daughter, about the horrible nightmares she had had about Rachel. Nor had she been able to forget that day she was at the deathbed of Daniel Phenwick:

*Slowly Danny's eyes came open. Glazed, almost mystical in appearance. A dim smile, a yellowish-*

*white light illuminating his face. "Rachel? Rachel, you mustn't blame me." The pupils rolled toward Rebecca. "I did the best I could, Rachel. You'll understand in time—I'm just beginning to understand." He weakly reached for her hand. "When I was young—oh, that was so long ago—I thought I never wanted to have children. I love all three of my sons, but was afraid of you, Rachel—you were the only girl."*

*I'm not Rachel, Grandfather," she said softly.*

*Danny vacantly chuckled. "Oh, but you are, my child."*

*"I'm Rebecca, your son Elias' daughter."*

*"Rebecca—Rachel—one and the same." He gazed about, not recognizing the other faces staring into his. "I'm at Phenwick House again, aren't I?"*

*"Yes." Mike clung tightly to his other hand.*

*"Ah, my dearest friend, Mickey. You must stay behind. I want you to promise that you will see that Phenwick House goes to my Rachel . . . Will you promise, Mickey? Will you take care of Rachel, look after her?"*

*"I think you mean Rebecca, don't you, Danny?"*

*"Rebecca—yes—Rebecca . . ." Danny's face glowed and a smile of peace came over him, his eyes staring into infinity.*

In her heart of hearts, Rebecca knew that her grandfather had believed she was Rachel reincarnated. The evidence strongly pointed that way.

"What are you thinking, Mother?" Kate asked.

"Nothing of any importance, Kate Phenwick," Rebecca answered.

"Do you believe I'm going mad like Cousin Rachel?" Kate asked.

Rebecca turned with a startled expression. Kate had never before seen such anger come to her mother's face, nor had she ever known her to lose her temper so quickly. "Cousin Rachel was not mad! She was possessed by alien spirits that wanted to use her body! But she was not mad, nor are you!"

"Mother?" Kate looked aghast.

"I thought I had long ago heard the end of Cousin Rachel," Rebecca continued. "Am I to be haunted by her all my days?"

"Mother—please don't be angry with me. I'm only trying to understand the terrible thing that happened to me," Kate half-moaned as she was on the verge of tears.

Wild eyes stared at her daughter before Rebecca regained control. As she realized what had happened, the woman went to the child with open arms. "Oh, Kate Phenwick! Forgive me. I don't know what suddenly came over me." They were face to face. "If at anyone, I'm angry at myself. I don't want to be the reincarnation of Rachel; but there are those who think that I am. I even believe my beloved Johnny Ornby thought I was, and there were times when I have no doubt my own precious father believed it, too. You've brought a copy of Rosea Hackleby's book into this house, although I swore I would never read it. I will never open the cover of that book because, to be perfectly honest, I don't want to know who I was—*if* indeed I did live before."

"Oh, Mother, I'm terribly sorry," Kate returned, clinging fast to the woman. "I had no idea that you would be so disturbed about this. But—" She caught herself.

Rebecca did not alter her position. Her eyes searched beyond her daughter as she felt her desperate embrace. Kate Phenwick needed help; Rebecca might well be the only one who could assist her. She must swallow her own emotions and do her best to comprehend. "But *what*, Kate Phenwick? What's troubling you?"

"When I saw that terrible thing happening in the basement room at Falmouth House," Kate said hesitantly, "I had the distinct sensation—or perhaps I should say *realization*, that I was or had been one of the two parties involved." A sob wiggled up from deep within her. She cried, it was easier than putting her thoughts into words.

"There, there, Kate Phenwick," Rebecca returned. Again she swallowed hard to conquer her own terrible emotions of that moment. "You're thinking that if I had been—let us say—Rachel, then you would have been—I can't say it. It's too preposterous an idea." She held Kate tighter, if that were possible. "Yet from the very beginning, from the moment you were born—even while I was carrying you—I had such a deep feeling of love for you. How else can I express it? My mother used to say I had an abnormal love for you. She thought I was spoiling you by doting over you. Mother never considered me, nor did I think of myself, as a very feminine child. I was not the type who appreciated ruffles and dolls. I wanted to ride and play with toy soldiers and boats. At *La Chenille* I used to bully the other girls and several times I got into minor problems. In other words, I wasn't the type to fawn over a baby the way I did. I desperately wanted to have you. Although it made no difference whatsoever, I confess, I was a bit disappointed when you turned out to be a girl. I always thought I could have dealt better with a boy. But once you had arrived, I knew I could never love any child the way I loved you. My first husband, Johnny Ornby, used to hide his disappointment that I had not had a child by him. He was extremely intuitive and the only man I ever knew who admitted that he had communicated with Grandmother Augusta."

"Did you ever feel a closeness to Grandfather Danny?" Kate managed to ask after she had controlled her sobbing.

"I had a singular attraction to him," Rebecca admitted. "He was always mysterious and kept to himself. Yes, I would have to admit that I had a remarkable relationship with the man. When my life was threatened that time by Moab whatever his name was, the black man, I instinctively felt it would be Grandfather who would come and save me. Why I thought that I'll never know." She stroked her daughter's hair. "Whatever the past was—whatever reason you were born, my child—I don't feel is really important. The only thing that is is that you are mine for whatever reason the Almighty brought us together. If we did live other lives—and I don't know that I will ever be convinced of that—then I am happy they have brought us to where we are at this moment."

"I couldn't ever want a sweeter, dearer mother," Kate replied, kissing her on the cheek. She would control the many questions that had risen in her mind and not disturb her mother beyond what she already had.

Fortunately Ella Shane appeared at that moment. She was her usual cheery, smiling self. "If we're going to prayer meeting this evening, Mrs. Phenwick, we're going to have to think about fixing dinner. Your cousin, Jane Augusta, has made several broad hints about food. I can tell she's working up an appetite."

"Will you go to prayer meeting with us tonight, Kate Phenwick?" her mother asked, disengaging herself from the prolonged embrace.

"Must I, Mother? If Cousin Jane Augusta doesn't go, I would rather stay with her," Kate replied.

"Whatever you prefer, my dearest. Now go see if you can persuade Jane Augusta to stay home," Rebecca said lightly, sending the girl from the room.

Ella Shane watched the girl run from the room. She could not help but notice that her eyes were red. "Problems?"

"What would life be if we didn't have problems to break up the monotony of a placid routine?" Rebecca asked, now able to smile. "I wonder if it wasn't a mistake to send Kate Phenwick to Falmouth House with Lydia. Still I could not bear the thought of returning to that terrible house. I didn't realize it would have such a negative effect upon my daughter as well." She sighed. "Well, it's done with. Come along, Ella, let us invade the kitchen with an idea or two about supper."

The library was in the rear part of Phenwick House. On the long evenings of summer, it was the last room to get dark. As far as Kate was concerned it was the friendliest room in the entire house. No portraits hung it, only two landscape scenes painted in oil. Tranquillity emanated from the room. It was comfortable.

Kate had lit two oil lamps at the table. She had gotten down a book of her Grandmother Patricia's poetry, a favorite reading pastime.

Jane Augusta entered the room, picking her teeth with a straw. "I don't know why I was hesitant in telling this while your mother was here," she began, "but I spent a while this afternoon snooping around the old cottage on the cliff."

"Uncle Mike's cottage?" asked Kate.

"Yes, the one he built," Jane Augusta returned. "Uncle Uriah lived in it after Michael O'Plaggerty went to his great reward. He had a housekeeper tend it for him. No one has lived there since Uncle Uriah's death. Still the place is kept immaculately clean. That portrait of your mother is still hanging there. The one signed by Michel O'Plaggerty. Not to be mistaken for Uncle Mike,

Michel was his nephew, son of his brother Kelly. He was a no-good one. Left a wife and children here in Greenfield, had another in Boston. Goodness knows how many others he had scattered around the countryside. Still he was a very good painter. Your mother tells me she doesn't much care for the painting because, while it is of her head and face, it has the body of a girl who was one of her best friends at the time."

"I used to play in the cottage when I was a child. It was a place I used to go to escape. Oh, the romantic dreams I used to conjure up there," Kate commented. "I don't know why I don't go there anymore."

Jane Augusta went to the library shelf and extracted the book compiled from the writings of Rosea Hackleby. "Your mother isn't too pleased having this book at Phenwick House, is she?"

"I think she has a kind of fear of it," Kate replied. "Afraid that she might discover something she doesn't want to know about."

"I showed her the section dealing with the possession of Rachel Phenwick," Jane Augusta commented, "and she flew all into a rage. I confess I don't understand what motivated her to do that."

Kate's curiosity was up. "Show me the section."

"I've got it located with a marker," Jane Augusta said, opening the book to the exact page. "There are seven pages about it. Rosea Hackleby must have been living at Phenwick House most of the time, or at least she gathered a lot of information about the poor unfortunate child."

Kate was reading. "Rachel attacked Uncle Mike. Apparently he was one of the first to witness her mysterious affliction." She read further. "I must say Rosea Hackleby must have been obsessed by the idea of reincarnation and the belief in the relationship people have with one another from life to life. I find it all very eerie—but curious."

"Curious?"

"Kate, the curious ... remember? That's me."

"It's good to have a curious mind, Kate, as long as it is open and receptive to new ideas. But how could it be otherwise?"

After finishing the section about Rachel and going back to read several paragraphs a second time, Kate closed the book. "Maybe my curiosity will get the better of me, but I have an uncanny desire to discover the truth—if it can be found—about this whole situation."

"Perhaps you should return with me to Boston, Kate," Jane Augusta suggested. "I think you might find my brother, Theodore—Dr. Ted—interesting. He gets very much involved in Rosea's writings and believes there is sufficient validity to them."

"Cousin Theodore?" Kate questioned. "It seems I heard Nancy Phenwick mention him several times."

"He has been the family doctor for years," Jane Augusta explained. "He is just younger than I am. He has delivered all four of Nancy's sons. And fine healthy lads they are. More than a general practitioner, he is deeply interested in the mind. What is it they call it? Psychology? His own son Augustus—not to be confused with the late Gus Phenwick—is now in Europe studying with doctors who specialize in the working of the mind and the personality. I don't understand a thing about it, but Augustus would. He's always been that type of a boy. Another son, Joseph, my eldest nephew, is also interested in the subject. Ted was able to help Harriet Cox before she married Prentise by putting her under something called hypnotism or some such word. You'd have to speak with him to get the whole gist of the subject. I confess I'm blank when it comes to technical terms."

"I think I would like to go meet Cousin Theodore," Kate said softly. "Besides, I would also like to visit Grandmother Patricia again. As Lydia said, a girl can't expect to meet any worthwhile men in Greenfield. And I have a feeling about Boston. He—whoever the he is for me—might be there."

# CHAPTER TWELVE

Dr. Theodore Ornby was a tall man with distinguishing features. Brown hair and beard that were turning gray. He possessed a well-constructed body which had altered little over the years. His voice was deep, resonant and had a way of penetrating into a person's mind. While he continued his regular medical practice in Boston, he became more and more select with the number of patients with whom he dealt. His preference went to those who seemed to have psychosomatic disturbances, occurring from some abnormality of their minds. An open person, he inspired confidence in his patients, treating them whether on a physical or mental level as an old country doctor might. He gave them confidence to disclose the problems which were disturbing them. Continually he discovered that many of the illnesses presented to him were caused by faulty mental conditions, beliefs in sickness and repressed memories of past experiences which somehow haunted the individual, ultimately causing him to become physically distressed. While not recognized as a practicing psychologist by authorities in the field, he had had sufficient study in Europe to well qualify him. Ultimately he desired that his sons Joseph and Augustus, would be far better equipped to handle situations he considered to be brought about by mental disorders.

The office was modestly furnished. The large room which was his principal working area had a desk, three chairs and a covered pallet, resembling a chaise, slightly inclined to allow the patient not to be completely flat. The decor of the office was simple. The walls were white above oaken paneling. Pictures of serene countrysides were mounted above the woodwork. A congenial atmosphere permeated the chamber, quite like other doctors' offices. Clutter was kept to a minimum.

Jane Augusta had had a dinner at her home to introduce Dr. Ted to Kate Phenwick Cathcart. The occasion was one of light humor and family chatting. Dr. Ted took an interest in the girl, first and foremost from his earlier conversation with Jane Augusta. They had an immediate rapport. Although she was somewhat confused, the girl's curious nature proved to be open to new discoveries.

On the day Kate went to Dr. Ted's office, she was accompanied by Jane Augusta. The doctor's sister was surprised to learn her presence was not wanted during the interview. Kindly Dr. Ted informed her that she could either wait outside or come back in an hour.

Jane Augusta tried not to leave in a huff, but she was disgruntled at being ejected from her brother's office. She felt she had a personal interest in the matter and should be allowed to be present.

"Now then, my dear Kate," Dr. Ted began, "if you

will take a seat we will simply have a conversation, shall we?"

"Whatever you say, Doctor," she answered, taking a chair opposite the doctor's desk.

Ted leaned back and placed the tips of his fingers together as he observed her. "What we are about to do is a relatively new form of science, Kate. It is yet an infant, being experimented with in some of the larger cities of Europe. My knowledge is limited. Although my technique is not the most advanced, I will do all I can to help you unravel the distorted images that are coming to your mind."

"I admit I'm a bit reluctant to go through with this, Dr. Ted," she said softly. "The experience I had at Falmouth House was quite upsetting and the memory of it had been haunting me ever since."

"In that case, why don't you describe it to me?" Dr. Ted suggested. "We have found that one of the basic treatments in dealing with matters of the mind is to bring the problem out in the open that we may examine why it has presented itself in the first place. It's no different than if I were diagnosing an appendicitis or a case of measles. I would have to know the why and wherefore of the patient's condition. In this case we're dealing with something that is in your head."

Kate related the entire experience she had had in the basement at Falmouth House. Later she told of the conversation she had had with her mother in which Rebecca had admitted that there were those who believed she was the reincarnation of Rachel Phenwick.

"Yes, I have read the account according to Rosea Hackleby about Rachel," Dr. Ted commented after listening for several minutes without interruption. "As a matter of fact while I was quite a young man, I discussed the incidents concerning our late relative with

Rosea. The lady was in her last years then. Her mind at times, although generally clear, was hazy on certain facts that were contradictory and disturbing. Since the time she first wrote about Rachel, she had had other thoughts on the matter and said that she wished to abridge her original writings. I don't believe she did that, and the printed edition we have is the original version. I suspect she was more accurate in the beginning than she was in later years when time had gotten between her and the event. No doubt her own conjecture had somehow sullied her opinions."

"Do you believe in reincarnation, Dr. Ted?" Kate asked, crossing her legs and appearing restless.

"I don't say that I do, and I don't say that I don't," the doctor replied. "I find it is all very interesting, which is the only way one can approach any matter of the occult. We can obtain no proof. Therefore we go on a kind of acceptance through faith, or through evidence of our own—what shall I say—inner perceptivity. For the sake of hypothesis, let us take the present attitude that there is a reality to reincarnation. Now, according to Rosea—and I don't know the exact quote—she proclaims that the reason for reincarnation is for the spirit or soul to learn from various lifetimes, as well as during the time between body incarnations. In the Eastern belief a matter of karma is projected. That is, one is as one is because one was as one was. That involves many consequences in logic. It means, because we have encountered, say, a compatible soul or entity in another lifetime, we are liable to meet that entity again and again over a period of many lifetimes. One of the reasons for this is that we have different relationships with each other. For example, Jane Augusta and I may have been together, according to Rosea's theory, in several different lifetimes. At one time my soul might have done her a wrong, albeit small or great as the case may be. We may not have been related, and for most of that lifetime complete strangers. We came together—say we were both men at that time—and we had a conflict, a duel, and one of us wounded the other or even killed him. As a result we would have a negative karmic tie one with the other. Because I had done her a wrong, or vice versa—it takes two to play in a game—we had to come back maybe several times to make up for that wrong."

"I don't believe I understand all this, Dr. Ted."

"Don't attempt to comprehend, my dear," he said kindly. "Just listen and you will pick up anything that is pertinent to you. Do you understand?"

"Yes."

"I will continue. Now suppose that this karmic debt I had with Jane Augusta was such that it could only be satisfied by an expression of love, not necessarily a husband and wife romantic love; but only through the kind of love that can develop between a brother and sister. Do you see what I mean?"

"I believe so."

"Good. Let's take another example. You have heard of the case of Lillian Phenwick, have you not?"

"Yes. She practiced voodoo on Nancy and was burned alive in an old house."

"Precisely. Lillian had created a karmic situation for herself. Perhaps it had been established many lives ago. It was something she had to play out with Nancy: some antagonism. Or there's a good chance they never met previously; thus, because of what she did in this life, she has made a karmic situation that she will have to come back again to erase."

"Wouldn't a person like that go to Hell?" Kate asked.

Dr. Ted sat back and chuckled, his fingertips tapping together as he laughed. "I must confess with all due respects to Lillian, her son Gordon and the fundamentalist church, I don't much believe in that old theory of Heaven and Hell. That's why I'm inclined to believe in the principle of reincarnation. It makes more sense and it's not quite as gory when you analyze it. You see, Lillian may well come back as a close friend or a child of Nancy's. This may not happen again for another hundred to a thousand years, according to Rosea. Yet there are lives that exist at the same time in a kind of close bond that are different in the respect that— Say a person has a child in one life, and doesn't quite fulfill his destiny as a parent; in another life, to make up for that, the situation is reversed and the child then becomes the parent to the one who had been the parent in the former life. Perhaps this is not clear, Kate. It has a kind of logic to me that is not always easy to communicate to others."

"I think I'm beginning to understand a little of which you're speaking," Kate replied, feeling a little less uneasy. "Let's say, for instance, in a previous life—this is difficult for me to say—that I had had a child. Well—say, for instance, that I had been Daniel Phenwick and the child I had was Rachel. As Daniel I had not been a particularly good father to my daughter, resulting in the situation wherein Rachel felt some kind of emotional lack to the point that she became susceptible to—what did Rosea call them?—alien forces. Once the alien forces had taken over, they tried to get back at Daniel."

"Pardon if I interrupt," Dr. Ted inserted, leaning forward at his desk to gaze into the girl's face. "I think that by introducing the element of the alien spirits, we are bringing in other entities. You were on the right line of thought in the beginning by thinking that because Daniel had neglected his daughter, that created a tie. Let us assume that one of her reasons for the problem was that she had lacked love from her father. Probably also the lack of attention of love she needed from her mother. Because her father was away so often, she became disturbed."

"I see what you mean. Although it may have been a cause for her weakening, it wasn't *the* cause that attracted the alien spirits to her."

"Precisely."

"If—and I don't even like to think it—if my mother is the reincarnation of Rachel, because of that unfortunate relationship with her father, his spirit might have returned in the form of her child. She made up, as mother, for the lack of love she had received as a former child. Is that what you're saying?"

"I think you pretty much have the point," Dr. Ted commented. "If such were the case, it has put you and your mother in a very close relationship wherein a very deep love exists between you. Not that a deep love did not exist between Daniel and Rachel—it did, but it had been distorted. Now the situation has been reversed. You express your love to each other in a much closer way."

"Supposing that is true, Dr. Ted," Kate stated, "why would Danny not come back again as a male child? After all, my mother dearly preferred to have a boy—she's admitted that to me."

"Again I have to go back to something Rosea told me and is not included in the book," Dr. Ted confided. "The entity or the soul, whatever you want to call it, takes on the physical body that best helps it express itself during a particular lifetime. You, no doubt, had other ties with various souls. Perhaps many of them have not reincarnated again. Still there may be one or two who have. Those particular entities may appear as—say for instance—a husband, lover or children. There may be any number who appear as children. Perhaps there are those who have come back as friends—that of course is hypothetical and without foundation."

"You mean that whatever the relationship was between father and daughter may have been evolved, but that other relations are still to be worked out?"

"That would seem to be the case if there is any validity to this theory at all, Kate." Dr. Ted rose and paced to the window, pushing it open that he might permit more air into the room. An afternoon breeze was rustling the elm outside. A pleasant sweetness wafted into the room. "What are you thinking, Kate?"

"That I don't know whether I believe in any of this or not, Cousin Theodore," the girl replied, sitting quietly in the chair, her hands folded sedately in her lap.

"I rather imagine that you don't—which is just as well," Dr. Ted returned, looking back at her. "I would be disappointed if you did. Yet you have food for thought."

"Why am I being haunted so by all of this? Why do I sometimes think I'm going mad?" Kate questioned, a frantic expression portraying her emotions.

"Because something, somewhere, is trying to help you work out whatever problem you have," Dr. Ted said, going to where the girl was sitting and propping himself against the desk. "Let me assure you, Kate Phenwick, that you're not going mad. You are disturbed and with good reason. But you are far from going mad, so put that out of your mind. If in time you do not sort out these thoughts and find some logical reason behind them, they could well affect your personality and your mental state in years to come. You have no doubt read or heard of the ambition of Augusta Phenwick—a woman I never met, but for whom I have admiration—and her desire to watch over the Phenwick women. I imagine she's doing that, although it may be detrimental to her own progress. Still it may be part of her own karmic thing to experience what she's going through."

"I've heard of Great-grandmother Augusta and the alleged fact that her spirit lingers about," Kate admitted. "I don't know if I've felt it, or if I should have. Why did you ask?"

"I was curious to know of how much you were aware," Dr. Ted replied. He pushed himself up and walked around to behind his desk. "In time, my dear, I would like to try some experiments with you, if you don't mind. Perhaps a little hypnosis to see if you can be regressed back in time."

"I don't know that I would want to experience that."

"You would be completely unaware of anything other than just a calm, wonderful, relaxing rest. You would not be aware of anything that was happening. I assure you that I would tell you nothing that was detrimental or harmful in any way. But it might be a way for us to discover part of your past. I am curious. Again going on the presumption that you might be the reincarnation of Daniel Phenwick—and that is strictly a conjecture—I am wondering what other persons might have returned in this lifetime to be with you."

"I am not ready to accept that I was once my own great-grandfather," Kate said.

"Of course, you're not," Dr. Ted returned with authority. "I would not expect you to be. However, I am curious to know if there is any other person to whom you have had a reaction, either through encounter, or by remembering their names or speaking of them."

"I don't understand what you mean," Kate remarked.

"For instance, when you saw the picture of Uncle Danny at Phenwick House and at Falmouth House, you had a definite feeling of reaction, did you not?"

"Yes."

"And when you saw the Rachel—that terrible thing that Grandmother insisted on keeping in the music room, why I will never know—you had another cringing reaction, didn't you?"

"Yes, I told you that."

"I remember." Again Dr. Ted tapped his fingertips together, bringing them close to his beard and catching strands of hair as he did so. "Did you have any particular reaction to the portrait of Edward Phenwick?"

"At one point I sensed a certain feeling of compassion for him, but it was nothing like the reaction I had to the others."

"Compassion? A good word," Dr. Ted commented. "Were there any other portraits that affected you?"

"None that I can think of."

"Were there any names mentioned that caused you to have a prickly reaction when they were spoken?" Dr. Ted asked.

"No, I can't—" She stopped. "There is one that gives me an eerie feeling."

"Good. Whose name is it?"

"Uncle Michael's," Kate replied. "I think it just a coincidence. After all, he wasn't a member of the family."

"Uncle Michael?" Ted scratched his beard. "Ah, yes, Michael O something or other, wasn't it?"

"Michael O'Plaggerty."

"Oh yes, I recall, he was the son of an indentured slave that Augusta Phenwick brought over from England."

"He was also the brother of Margaret Phenwick, Daniel's wife."

"Ah yes, now I recollect where I heard about him," Ted exclaimed. "And what about Margaret? What do you feel toward her?"

"Nothing in particular. I feel a little sad about her. I

don't have any queer sensations when her name is mentioned, or when I've seen her portrait."

"Very well. Let us go back to Michael O'Plaggerty. What does the name suggest to you?"

"Warmth. Closeness. A—a kind of love, I would say," Kate replied.

"As I recall, Michael O'Plaggerty was a very close friend of Uncle Danny's, was he not?" asked Dr. Ted.

"I've heard that Michael was quite fond of him," Kate returned, "that Danny practically died in his arms."

"I recall that, too, along with Rosea's interpretation of it," Dr. Ted commented.

"What *was* her interpretation?" That prickly sensation was moving over her back.

"Acute friendship. The love of one friend for another, a Damon and Pythias sort of thing, if you know anything about Greek mythology; or Jonathan and David, as in the Bible. Very close friends, entities who had come together and probably had been together many lives before. In that particular life, according to Rosea, she believed they were to live out existences as good friends, which is a degree of love that we don't generally speak about. Friendship is not considered on the same terms as matrimonial relationships. Again, according to Rosea, she believed the two men had karmic ties they had to work out *only* as friends—nothing more. They expressed themselves in that kind of relationship for what it was. Furthermore, she thought that one day they would come back again in a different type of love relationship; perhaps one that was demonstrated in more of a physical way. Do I make myself clear?"

"I believe so," Kate replied. "Aren't you suggesting that one day I might—or that is, that Danny might encounter his old friend again, only this time they would have a different type of relationship?"

145

"That could well be why one would appear in a following lifetime as a man and the other as a woman," Ted remarked. "I hope I haven't confused you too greatly, my dear cousin. In the days to come we will have other discussions such as this. I feel the fear you have of certain old houses has to do with some past existence—whoever you may have been. The sooner you become aware of that, the sooner you will experience a sense of freedom from whatever shadow is looming over from the past."

# CHAPTER THIRTEEN

1855

That winter had begun early and had become severe by January 1855. Boston received an unusual amount of snow, one blizzard immediately following the previous one, which caused the residents to remain indoors much more than they cared to. Businesses slowed. Even communication among families became remote. Kate had returned to Greenfield just prior to winter, where the weather was also severe.

The shipping industry was slowed practically to a standstill by the wintery conditions. Many of the companies refused to sail under such adverse conditions or were limited to a minimum amount of activity. Sailors were idle and jobs were scarce.

During those cold months Stuart Phenwick managed to spend as much time as possible with the lovely Marcia Phenwick, his adopted cousin. They were not related by blood, ergo assumed to be an ideal pair. Even old Patricia Phenwick approved of the relationship and encouraged it to the extent of her ability. Stuart could not hide his love for Marcia, nor she hers for him. With all the sophistication she had learned and practiced, she was like an ordinary schoolgirl in his presence. The other suitors who had come to call on her over the years were informed she had made up her mind and had no intention of changing it. Wedding plans were made for that spring.

By March the snows were still collected in large piles along the streets. The wind whipped up from the harbor, making the cold seem even colder than it was. Stuart began returning for longer periods of time to the Medallion office where he was making plans for future shipments. Some vessels were arriving at Boston harbor. The stevedores were back to work, often under treacherous conditions.

John Collier arrived on a ship from New York in mid-March. Winter was still predominate. He had little money with him, having banked his savings while in New York, and had no way of getting hold of them. Because he was in Boston, the destination which he had long striven to reach, he did not sign back aboard the vessel on which he had arrived. Work was difficult to find. Three times he went to the Medallion office. The clerk who interviewed informed him that there would be little sailing before the first of April. Then it would be unlikely that they would need men other than their regulars until mid-month or perhaps not until May.

"Is it possible for me to see Mr. Phenwick?" John asked.

"He's away at the present," was the curt reply. "He doesn't have personal contact with the seamen."

"If it's possible, I would like to see him."

"It is impossible."

"Can you tell me where he lives?" John persisted.

"That is against company regulations."

"Can you tell me where any of the Phenwick family live?"

"No, I cannot do that. The only hope is to wait around

"How will I know them?"

until one of them comes to the piers."

"That's your problem, isn't it, mister?" The man was annoyed. "Now if you will please to leave, I have much to do."

"Thank you, I will come back mid-month or later and see if anything has opened by then."

John left the pier and went along the shipping area to see if the other companies might have work. The answer was always the same. Immigrant labor was more than plentiful. He had made a mistake by not shipping back to New York, taking another month or two before he got back to Boston. At least in New York he would have had access to his money. His next problem was to find other work. The best to be offered was labor shoveling snow. It was necessary to keep the streets as clear as possible. He accepted the challenge.

What little money he had brought with him and the little they paid for the monotonous labor hardly kept him in sufficient means. He discovered most of the men who shoveled snow were either derelicts or very poor people, who knew avenues of getting assistance. There were missions established by the fundamentalist churches along the waterfront, which offered meager shelter, watery bean soup and dry bread; occasionally food of some substance but not very palatable was offered. Such benevolent hospitality always included a long evangelical sermon by a zealous preacher.

Out of desperation John went to such a mission. As he had heard, the food was on par with hog swill. The dregs of humanity, who relied on such sustenance, accepted it gratefully and listened to the emotionally fired sermons of the different ministers who came from their own churches to speak to the derelicts. How had John gotten into such a position? If only he could find a person with whom he could speak, he might be able to get a loan to finance his way back to get his own money. It was one of those circumstances which were difficult to explain and one which proved to be demeaning to the man.

The particular night that John Collier imbibed of the food and other hospitalities, the sermon was preached by a round-faced man, who looked well fed. The hellfire-and-damnation spouting was keyed at a base emotional level, appealing to the superstitious nature of man. The preacher's hands flailed the air, his shrieking tones pierced the ears. He screamed and hollered, stamped his feet and made so many dramatic gyrations that the performance alone was a moving experience. Afterward he beseeched the poor misguided humanity to accept an altar call, asking the sinful men to come forward, confess their Jesus and be saved.

The room smelled of coal smoke, wine and the stench of unbathed bodies. Pathetic faces with watery eyes stared up at the preacher, who appeared to be not without some form of opulence. Feet shuffled. Chairs creaked. Periodically a coughing fit from the audience would cause the preacher to increase his volume until he had worked himself into a divine frenzy.

John was moved by the performance, almost becoming tempted to heed the man's verbose cry for confession. But what had he done wrong? He could think of nothing except that he did not embrace the tenets proclaimed by the dogmatic orator and self-proclaimed evangelist. He waited on the hard chair while the other sniveling men went forward to present themselves for confession of faith and receive the elegant minister's blessings. John attempted to comprehend what these people hoped to gain by blatantly reacting to the machinations of the man. Perhaps it would get them a better bed in which to sleep that night instead of merely a tattered blanket and a place on the crowded dormitory floor. He guessed that most would return to their sinning—whatever it had been—once the ordeal of the night was over and they saw the light of the next day. He supposed there would be those who would be transformed for a short period of time, maybe others for longer durations.

When the last of the tattered men left the altar and had been attended by devout missionaries, the preacher looked up. He stared with fierce eyes beneath heavy eyebrows and glared directly into John Collier's face. Wiping a pudgy hand with well-cleaned fingernails over his full face and square jaw, the relatively young man gathered his notes. Not more than thirty, his corpulent appearance made him appear younger than his actual age. He beckoned to John, who remained where he was seated. A challenge was presented. The preacher left the pulpit and strutted down to where John was sitting.

"Would you like me to pray for you, my son?" asked the man in a pompous, self-righteous voice.

"It seems you did enough praying for me earlier, Reverend," John replied, trying not to sound impudent. "I was merely sitting here observing the spectacle, wondering what this was all about. It's quite a show."

"You don't sound like a derelict," the preacher said suspiciously.

"I am not a derelict," John replied. "I'm a little down on my luck. I happen to have left my money in New York at a bank. I arrived in Boston with little cash.

Thinking there would be work, I naturally did not carry a lot of money with me. It's not safe to travel at sea with an unusual amount or more than necessary funds. I didn't realize I would get stranded in Boston."

"So you've come to this! Why don't you confess your Jesus and be saved?" the preacher asked.

"Be saved from what?" John questioned. "The cold outside? I don't think your approach is necessary to my salvation. I don't mean to be unkind, sir, I'm merely saying that—while I was impressed by your dramatic gyrations, and I admit I was moved by the performance—what you had to say was not in accord with my way of thinking."

The preacher put his hand on John's shoulder. "I would like to help you if you would be saved."

"If you believe so greatly in the teachings of Jesus Christ and are such a staunch Christian, why would you not want to assist me even if I were not saved?" John inquired.

"I beg your pardon?" The man blinked, then enlarged his eyes again to that fierce expression he wore so effectively at the pulpit. "Did I hear you rightly?"

"Yes. I questioned your motive for being a Christian," John stated. "Is it all for show and pomposity? Or do you really believe in helping people to help themselves? You would get further with me if you were to guide me to find myself physically, to get a job that would pay enough to get a room of sufficient comfort and food to feed myself, that I would not have to rely on the beneficence of such missions as this. Then I would truly believe you were a man of God, Reverend."

"Blasphemy!"

"Is it? I don't think so. It seems to me it's being practical and to the point," John said with a pleasant smile.

The preacher did not know how to react. "You speak with an educated vocabulary."

"I am self-taught."

"All the more reason to be appreciated." He took a card from his pocket and scribbled a name and address upon it. Handing it to John, he said, "You will spend the night in this place of God, among this degenerate humanity. Bathe in the morning, then present yourself at my office no later than ten o'clock. I accept your challenge. If you cannot find the address, someone will surely give you directions. God bless you, sinner." He hurriedly left the foul-smelling room.

John chuckled to himself and watched as the preacher made a somewhat theatrical exit. When his amusement had subsided, he glanced down at the card, the address, the man's name. "Reverend Gordon Phenwick." He said the name out loud. "Repent and be saved." Had he accidentally stumbled onto a member of *the* Phenwick family? He would make a point of being at the church very early the next morning.

Although Gordon Phenwick was not especially busy the next day, he required John Collier to wait three quarters of an hour before he was invited into the preacher's office. John had got his seabag and had changed into his best suit of clothing. He hardly looked like a derelict or a man who was desperately in need of work.

When Gordon saw him he was surprised; it was difficult to believe that he was the same man he had seen the night before in the mission.

John explained that he was a seaman, that he wanted work. He would be very happy to get any kind of job along the wharves.

"You informed me last night that you were self-educated," Gordon remarked. "Do you do any kind of book work?"

"I read and write and do figures," John replied.

"A strange coincidence. Last night I was visiting with my brother—a man who is not totally disposed to my own way of thinking. He happens to be my only brother, therefore I have communication with him. He mentioned he needed a man who could handle figures at the Medallion office. His clerk has recently taken ill. It would be a temporary job—perhaps for only a few weeks. It would certainly help you to get established. Have you reconsidered your salvation?"

"Does that make a difference as to whether I get to interview for the job?"

Gordon puffed his cheeks, then exploded air. "I suppose it shouldn't have any bearing on the matter, should it? Very well, I'll give you this card. You may take it to the person in charge of the Medallion office and tell him that Reverend Gordon Phenwick sent you. It's about the job of which my brother spoke last night. However, I hope you will seek your way to salvation before too long, my friend. It is a pity to remain a lost lamb all your life."

"I do not intend to remain a lost lamb all my life, sir. I plan to make something of myself and I expect to do it to the fullest of my ability. Thank you very much for this introduction. I've been to the Medallion office. They had no work when I was there. I'll try again, Reverend Phenwick. And thank you for your kindness."

"God go with you, my son. Think on what I told you. Your soul could burn in eternal flames if you're not careful."

"I'll be very careful, thank you."

John left the church office and went directly to the Medallion company. Before noon he was hired as a clerk to check the incoming goods on a ship that would arrive the next day. The work would also include certain office tasks, and he believed the position was an improvement upon his former way of life. He was closer to the family than he had been before. His next step was to meet the notorious Patricia—*if* she were still living.

Despite the brisk wind that swept over the harbor, John strolled along the piers. The cutting cold had a refreshing bite to it, as an ebullient feeling came over him. Staring down at the icy water, a series of pictures was projected into his mind's eye depicting the scenes of his past including before when he left home in Illinois. He had come a long way. Determination had got him this far, faith and confidence would get him the rest of the way. Waiting would only make the prize all the greater.

# CHAPTER FOURTEEN

John Collier learned rapidly. Within a week, he not only knew his own assignment but was well into learning the overall workings of the Medallion office. He saw many places where improvement could be made in procedures to enhance the efficiency and accuracy of the work. Reserving his suggestions, he watched, studied and waited. To bring up such matters to subordinates might appear as a criticism of them personally, and he did not want to stir any antagonism among his fellow workers.

The first week was a struggle and he had to draw from the foreman on his first week's wages to live. He obtained a small room and rationed his food that he might conserve every penny he had. The second week was not much easier since he had already spent half of his pay the week before. Yet that period of austerity was good for him, giving him a greater sense of values and the need to get ahead.

By the first week of April the snows had fairly much melted and the weather had begun to warm. A feeling of spring lifted John Collier's spirits. He seemed to be filled with new ambition and just a little anxious to advance himself beyond his present position.

While John sometimes enjoyed the company of men, he was certainly not in any way physically attracted to them. He observed women, but refused to indulge in the lusty speculation of other men. He had had experiences with women while traveling with Clarence Hoskins; but he would not allow himself to become a person of wanton morals. As the weather got nicer, more and more women appeared on the streets, some even ventured down by the docks. John admired them, momentarily speculated, but quickly put his thoughts to other matters.

Many times John questioned the validity of the notes Clarence Hoskins had taken while John was allegedly under hypnosis back in Quincy. His desire was to find another hypnotist and see if he could be put under again. If so, he would be curious to see if the notes from that occasion would match with those from the former.

The idea of a soul mate intrigued the young man and had caused him to speculate on many a romantic dream. Yet, if Clarence Hoskins got the notes correct, his soul mate was someone by the name of Danny. A man? At that time, he had been Michael—another man. But they were just friends—friends from childhood. If only he could speak with someone who knew about such things, or who even merely speculated about them. But who in that day and age did? Certainly nobody in the churches, and it seemed to him that it was a matter of spiritual nature. His one prayer was that his soul mate, whoever it was, would be a woman in this life. He believed in his heart of hearts that it must be. For he was certain he was magnetically moving toward that soul mate again.

Often John would become lost in dreamy speculation about the future. Yet in all his travels he had not been able to find anyone with whom he would speak who was an authority on such matters. Fact is, he could not discover anyone who took him seriously when he mentioned that he was idealistically waiting for his soul mate. He stopped mentioning it, holding his thoughts inward. If only there was someone. At one point he thought of going to visit Gordon Phenwick and broaching the subject to him. Quickly he decided against such a move since he only too well realized the kind of person the preacher was.

By then John had learned where Edward House was located. He was reluctant to try to get an interview with the grand old matriarch of the family without a proper introduction. He did not believe that the simple mention of Clarence Hoskins' name would get him admission.

Late on a lovely Thursday afternoon, the kind that made it seem spring had decided to stay for a while, John was busily checking a load of cotton that had arrived from Savannah. To get an accurate count, he had to climb up on several stacked bales. His position was precarious, but he felt he was agile enough to manage his way around. Suddenly he lost his footing and became wedged in between two bales, falling to waist level. It was a painful experience, and he cried out for help, although he realized that he was virtually alone on the dock at the time. The other men had gone home. Pushing and shoving, he merely managed to wedge himself deeper in among the bales. His foot was tangled on a rope and he could not maneuver his hands to get to it.

Again he called for assistance. Gulls squawked in reply. Desperately he attempted to push the bales of cotton away from him. He could not do it without help.

"Where are you? I can hear you calling," a voice yelled, "but I can't see you."

"Up here, between the bales of cotton."

"What are you doing up there?"

"I was trying to take a count and lost my footing," John returned. "If I could get a hand, I could probably hoist myself out. But I'm stuck and can't seem to get any leverage."

"Stay right there, I'll get a ladder."

"Where could I possibly go?" John asked with annoyance. "I'm afraid I'll turn my ankle if I'm not careful."

Within a few minutes, John could feel pressure against the bales and the movement of someone climbing up. "Over here."

"I brought a rope. Perhaps if you can get hold of it," the other said, crawling to where John was stuck.

John looked up into the handsome face of Stuart Phenwick. Immediate recognition. "I don't think I need the rope, Mr. Phenwick. Just give me your hand so I can get some leverage."

Automatically Stuart presented his hand in the fraternal handshake he had taught Gregory Phenwick years before in London. To him it was significant that their hands happened to meet in that way, thumbs and little fingers about each other.

"You know me," Stuart remarked with a grunt as he tugged to help, "but I don't seem to recall you."

John was out of the worst part of the position. It was then a matter of pulling upward with Stuart's assistance. Soon he was breathlessly seated on the bale, rubbing his ankle. "The name's John Collier."

Stuart stared at the man. "But I do know you. We've met before. Ah yes, I recall. It was in Savannah. You saved my life, Mr. Collier. I'm deeply indebted to you."

John grinned. "You see, the debt is repaid."

Both men laughed as Stuart sat on the bale opposite him. "Can I help you with your leg?"

"It's just my ankle," John replied. "It's a little tender, that's all. I don't believe I hurt it."

"If you think you should see a doctor, I can drive you to my Cousin Ted's place," Stuart offered. "He's one of the best you can find in Boston."

"That won't be necessary. Just let me get the circulation back in it and I'll continue with my work," John stated.

"Everyone else has gone home."

"I wanted to get this out of the way tonight. I've got the count—the hard way. All I have to do is total up the figures and do a little extra paper work," John said.

"John Collier? That name has a familiar sound to it. I don't believe you introduced yourself in Savannah. Fact is, you just suddenly disappeared, as I remember. Ah, John Collier! You're the man my foreman has mentioned. An exceptional man."

"I don't know about that, sir."

"Well, my foreman does. He says you could run Medallion single-handed."

"He exaggerates."

"Perhaps he does, then again—" Stuart sized the man up. "I should have known when you were working over the usual hours that you must be John Collier. Well, Mr. Collier, I'm pleased to make your acquaintance." Again he shook hands using the fraternal hold. John looked at their hands. "That's a special clasp of friendship, Mr. Collier."

"Sir, it doesn't sound right for you to call me Mr. Collier," John remarked. "I hardly know who you're speaking to. Couldn't you just call me John?"

"Certainly—if—?"

"If?"

"If you'll call me Stuart."

"I couldn't do that, Mr. Phenwick, you're—"

"I'm the owner of Medallion—that is, of the Boston office," Stuart returned. "So? That doesn't mean I don't enjoy friendship. And from what I've heard of you, and what I know of you from the past—I refer to Savannah—I think you are a person I would very much like to have as my friend, John."

"But Mr. Phenwick, I'm only—"

"Ah-ah! Stuart."

"Yes sir, Stuart, I'm only a common seaman. I've saved a few dollars and put them in a bank in New York, but I'm not the kind who should associate with the likes of you," John returned.

"Why not? Are you too good for me?"

"No. It's the other way around."

"No, John, you're mistaken." Stuart rubbed his face and sighed. "A man in my position has very few friends. Oh, I know a lot of people who try to get close to the affluent Phenwicks, but I have no really close men friends. Don't mistake my motives. I'm engaged to marry my foster-cousin, Marcia Phenwick. It's going to be a gala wedding in June."

"Congratulations, sir."

"Stuart."

"Stuart."

"Good." Stuart laughed. "I'm eagerly looking forward to the date. I've been in love with her for years. And I confess I've been faithful to that love. You know what I mean. The thing is, a man likes to have another man as a friend and confidant. Oh, I have relatives. My grandfather is very understanding, and, although he has a young wife, he is up in years. My brother Gordon—"

"I've met him—at the mission."

"Oh yes, that's right, you were the one. Coincidence." Stuart laughed.

John sneezed.

"God bless you!"

John sneezed again. "Where the thunder do you suppose the smell of violets is coming from?"

"God bless you again!" Stuart sniffed. "Violets? I don't smell—" He stopped short and cocked his head to study John's face. "You smelled violets?"

"Sure. Didn't you? They're gone now. Those darn things have made me sneeze ever since I was a boy back on the farm in Illinois," John related.

"My great-great-grandmother—" Stuart began.

"Augusta Phenwick?"

"You've heard of her?"

"Not really. I mean, an acquaintance of mine once mentioned the Phenwick name—that was back in Quincy, Illinois," John said, "and I just automatically responded by saying Augusta. I don't know where the name came from. And Clarence asked me how I knew about her. I told him I didn't."

"Come on, you're going to have supper with me, John," Stuart said, pushing to his knees and crawling toward the ladder. "And I'm not going to take no for an answer. Do you like seafood? I know a great restaurant not far from here. Where do you live? Close by? I'll go with you while you clean up and change your clothes. This is kind of a fancy place, and they like you to wear a suit."

"But Mr. Phen—I mean, Stuart—"

"I said I wasn't taking no for an answer."

The Pelican Restaurant was not altogether elegant, but it catered to a wealthy clientele. John Collier felt ill at ease in the place, walking behind Stuart and praying that his country-boy attitude would not embarrass the man who had brought him. Stuart ordered for both of them, including a bottle of rare wine.

"I'm not much of a drinker, Stuart," John informed the man when he poured the wine.

"Have a sip or two," Stuart coaxed. "After all, you went through a harrowing experience this afternoon being wedged in among the bales of cotton."

"It wasn't so bad." John laughed.

"As I was saying," Stuart continued a conversation he had begun earlier, "about my brother. Don't judge me by him. He's radical, a compulsive preacher. My mother was like that. Zealous is the word. Both of them."

"Your mother?"

"She's gone. Burned to death in an old house," Stuart said without emotion. "She brought it on herself. Ever since then I've not been devoutly religious. She was a hypocrite—and I suspect that Gordon is not far from being one. My father was entirely different. Dull, I think, is the word that best describes him. He's kind of like my Uncle Prentise down in Savannah. My father and Uncle Prentise were the dull Phenwick brothers, while Uncle Joshua and Aunt Joanna—their brother and sister—are just the opposite. I try to pattern myself after them—at least after Uncle Joshua. Grandfather Peter is a lot like Uncle Joshua. You can see where he gets his adventurous nature."

"You have quite a family."

"My wife-to-be, Marcia, is very much like Aunt Patricia—now there's a lady you'll have to meet!" Stuart exclaimed.

John could barely control his excitement. "Meet Patricia Phenwick?"

"She's getting on in years, but she's still a good old soul," Stuart commented. "She's the grand lady. That's what Marcia will be one day. One day? She is now. We're going to live at Edward House. Aunt Patricia has insisted we come to live there after the marriage."

"All of these names—" John sighed.

"At this moment they're only names. You'll meet them all," Stuart said. "I want you to know my family. I'll tell them you're a businessman I met in Savannah and that I've brought you up here to work with me at Medallion. They needn't know you used to be a checking clerk or a stevedore."

"*Used* to be?"

"Didn't I mention? I had been meaning to have a chat with you after the foreman was boastful about your work," Stuart continued. "I need a right-hand man, someone to help take on the extra work load because of the severe winter and a backlog of shipping. Grandfather used to work some with me, but he doesn't help anymore. I really need someone."

"And what makes you think I—?"

Stuart laughed. "Augusta told me."

"I beg your pardon."

Stuart laughed even louder. "I'll explain it to you sometime. I don't think you're ready for that right now."

"I'm confused."

"Don't be. Be happy," Stuart said, emptying a glass of wine and pouring himself another.

By the time the meal was concluding and tea was being served, they had discussed many different topics to discover they were in accord on most things.

"Why the troubled expression, John? Is there something bothering you?" Stuart asked after an awkward period of silence.

"There is a name that keeps coming to my mind,"

John answered. "I think I must have read about it somewhere."

"What name?"

"Danny."

"Danny? I have a Cousin Dan Ornby. He's an attorney," Stuart related. "He's a pretty good man to know. I suspect he was named for my great-grandfather."

"Your great-grandfather?"

"Daniel Phenwick. I never knew him, of course," Stuart said. "I've heard a few notorious stories about him. But he was basically a good man."

"Your great-grandfather?" John repeated. "There was also a Michael O something or other."

"Uncle Mike? That's another name I've only heard. You'd have to ask my grandfather about him," Stuart remarked. "I remember Cousin Jane Augusta speaking of him when Kate was down visiting last autumn."

A prickly sensation came over John. He sneezed.

"God bless you!"

"Kate?" John sneezed again.

"God bless you again!" Stuart said. "Another smell of violets?"

"Can you smell them?"

"No." Stuart laughed loudly. "Now I recall, Uncle Mike's last name was O'Plaggerty."

"Of course," John said as if he had made a tremendous revelation.

"How could one forget the name O'Plaggerty?"

It took a long time, John thought, but he did not say it aloud.

# CHAPTER FIFTEEN

A unique friendship developed in the acquaintanceship of Stuart Phenwick and John Collier. Almost immediately they were like old friends. Initially John felt out of place in the company of his wealthy associate, but with his craving for friendship, Stuart took the lead in the situation. During his early years, Stuart had been expected to be close to his brother. While at school, he had few chums largely due to his mother's domineering fundamentalist approach to religion. She projected her theories and beliefs to everyone her sons would bring to the house. Consequently he learned to rely on Gordon for companionship. His mother was also suspicious of the moral attitudes of boys Stuart's age and considered them bad influences.

Deprived of childhood friendships, it was no wonder when John Collier appeared that Stuart was open to establishing comradeship. No more had they met than

Stuart put John into a position of importance with Medallion Enterprises. Following that he invited John to come live at the Augustus Phenwick house. Since Gordon had taken an apartment years before, John could have his old room.

Within the week an outsider would have found it difficult to believe that Stuart and John had not been friends from boyhood. A kind of rapport developed that was enviable even to the best of friends. Stuart was elated. He could not do enough to make John feel at home in the rambling house where he had lived with only a small staff of servants for nearly six years.

John felt a remarkable kinship to Stuart. At first he thought perhaps his new friend was someone from the past, that his previous name might be among the notes Clarence Hoskins took that time in Quincy when Homer Dillsworth had him under hypnosis. Yet he did not feel he should pursue that trend of thinking at the present. Stuart was just a friend. He could put no more into it than that, nor should he. The fact that he was living in a comfortable home in a very good neighborhood made John feel as if he had stepped up in the world. Having a fine position with Medallion Enterprises made him believe that he was becoming more his own man and closer to his goals. As he went over those notes from the past, he could not disregard the name of the town of Greenfield, Maine, which seemed to protrude into his immediate plans. He knew for a fact that Phenwick House, the most notorious of all those houses constructed by Augusta Phenwick, was located there. He repeated Kate's name as if it had some kind of magical quality to it, looking forward to the time he would meet the young lady.

"We have an invitation for supper tonight," Stuart announced one beautiful spring afternoon when he popped into the Medallion office assigned to John Collier.

"*We* have?" asked John. "Where to tonight?"

"To meet my grandparents," Stuart replied with a twinkle in his eye. "They have invited us. I've told them all about you and they are anxious to meet you. Unfortunately Marcia cannot be with us. Rather than postpone the event to another time, they suggested that we make it tonight without her."

"What will I wear?"

"You have three new outfits of clothing since you've been living in my house," Stuart commented. "Surely among them you can find something suitable to wear to meet dear old grandparents."

"If you put it that way," John returned. "Still I don't know. Do you think it's all right? After all, they are your people."

"And you're *my* friend, John," Stuart said, "which makes my people your people. If I ever get to Illinois, I'll reverse the situation. How's that?"

"It's not the same. You're the wealthy Phenwicks. I'm just a seaman who happens to be well enough educated to fulfill a certain position at Medallion Enterprises."

"You're more than just a seaman," Stuart argued, "you're my friend. I don't want you ever to think that way again. Friendship is very important to me, and will be for as long as I live. Even after I'm married, and Marcia and I live at Phenwick House, I want you to stay on here and live in comfort with the servants."

"I can't afford this style of living," John objected. "You know that, Stuart."

"Nonsense. What is there to afford? You'll stay here as my guest."

"By myself?"

"There'll be servants."

"We'll come to that bridge when we get to it, won't we?" John remarked. "I feel like an opportunist, a person who has taken advantage of your good nature and disposition."

"If you have taken advantage of anything, it has been of my need for friendship," Stuart explained.

"What of Marcia? When am I to meet the mysterious lady?" John inquired.

"I had hoped you would meet her tonight. That was the purpose when I arranged with Nancy to have the supper," Stuart related. "Unfortunately Marcia could not make it. So it will just be the four of us."

"You call your grandmother Nancy?"

"Wait until you see her." Stuart laughed lightly. "We're going to dine with the Peter Phenwicks tonight, and you are going to be your charming self, John Collier. From there, who knows what important contacts you can make in Boston?"


"Go into the sitting room," Stuart instructed his friend as they entered the Peter Phenwick house. It was a lovely old mansion in one of the nicer parts of Boston. A recent acquisition, it had not always belonged in the family. After Peter's second marriage to Nancy Cox, he felt it would not be right for him to remain in the old family home. Nor would it be fair to his new wife to live among the old traditions and memories. She needed to set up her own house and become the mistress of it.

"Will you be long?" questioned John, feeling a bit uneasy in the strange place.

"No, I'm just going to have a word with my grandfather and see the children before they are put to bed," Stuart said.

"I'm certain to find something to amuse myself with in this spacious place."

John entered the sitting room as directed. He stared around at the opulent, rich draperies, the velvet-covered furniture, the wood that was highly polished and gorgeously carved. In that room was a portrait of Joanna Phenwick, Peter's only daughter. The actress was wearing a diamond tiara and a blue velvet gown that made her appear as royalty. Her beauty was astounding. John stood in amazement, admiring the features, the beautiful expression. Other pictures were about the room, most of them of landscapes and flowers. That was Joanna's room, in Peter's mind, and the only room for which he insisted upon having the choice of paintings. Nancy had not been averse to it, since she knew Joanna to be a charming, loving person.

The door burst open a few minutes later to reveal lovely Nancy Phenwick. She was wearing a red low-cut gown, trimmed with white. The satin skirt was wide and rustled with her movement. She wore diamonds. Her hair was nicely styled with long finger curls, which were fashionable. She looked like the southern belle that she was. Despite her twenty-nine years, she could have easily passed for a girl fresh from her teens, radiant for a party with a look of expectant wonder.

"I d'clare, is Mr. Phenwick in here?" she asked, only a trace of her southern accent remaining.

"I'm sorry, he's not. I'm here by myself," John said, somewhat overwhelmed by the lady.

"Now isn't that too bad," Nancy returned, batting her eyelashes. "I don't believe I know you. I'm Mrs. Phenwick. I suspect you must be Mr. John Collier." Her eyes glistened as brightly as her diamonds as she gazed at the man.

"I am John Collier, Miss Phenwick. I'm pleased to make your acquaintance." He obviously felt awkward in her presence. Believing it the proper thing to do, he clicked his heels and bowed.

Nancy giggled girlishly. "I'm Mrs. Phenwick, Mr. Collier. Mrs. Peter Phenwick." She laughed again. "I understand your startled expression. Stuart has gone and told you I was his grandmother, hasn't he? He does that to see how people will react. Actually, I am his grandmother now—I just don't look the part."

"I should say you don't." John had reddened.

"I'm surprised that either Stuart or Mr. Phenwick left you all by yourself in here," she continued, sweeping through the room as she went to rearrange the bouquet of roses on a large table by the window. "I simply love red roses, don't you? They're so fragrant and nice. Such beautiful colors, too. Mr. Phenwick is forever bringing them to me. He knows they're my favorite. He's such a sweet man." She meddled with the roses to cover her own nervousness. "Have you known Stuart long?"

The singularly handsome young man glanced away. "Why, in a sense, yes."

"In a sense? That does seem a peculiar choice of words, Mr. Collier," Nancy commented.

"I met Stuart in Savannah—some time ago," John said, only slightly stretching the truth. "He and I have recently become associated at Medallion."

"Oh, do you know Savannah, Mr. Collier?"

"I don't actually know the city. I've been there several times—but only in and out. My home is in Illinois, near Quincy."

"I don't believe I know Quincy," Nancy drawled, "and I don't even know where Illinois is. I'm really a little dense when it comes to geography, Mr. Collier. I have four children, you know. They occupy a great deal of my time. I suppose when they get to the age they have regular lessons and study about faraway places, I'm going to have to learn something about geography. Until that time I d'clare I'm not going to put myself out to acquire any knowledge about it." She laughed.

John had never seen a woman quite as beautiful as Nancy Phenwick. She radiated charm that he had known other southern women to possess. "You have four children, Mrs. Phenwick?" he asked, an incredulous expression coming to his face. "You don't look to be old enough to have one yet."

"You do flatter me, Mr. Collier. I find that amusing," Nancy commented. "To tell you the truth, I'm older than I look. And I do very definitely have four bright young boys. You must come and meet them sometime. There's Thadius Edward, John Samuel, Paul Raymond and Daniel Louis. One day they will all be married to Phenwick women. That's what I'm working toward, a whole group of Phenwick women to be my daughters-in-law."

"That's quite an ambition," John remarked.

"I do hope that the boys do well in life," Nancy said. "I'm very concerned about them. I want Mr. Phenwick to be proud of his sons—and pleased with my efforts. I do so dearly love the man, and his children are a godsend to me. You do understand, don't you, Mr. Collier?"

"I understand, Mrs. Phenwick."

A short while later Stuart appeared with his grandfather. His hair now snow-white and beginning to look more his age than he had even a few years back, Peter Phenwick walked with a hesitating step. Such infirmity annoyed him, for he had always been a strong, virile man, able to compete with others many years younger. He was proud of his physical prowess. Nearing seventy, time had slowed him to an irritating pace. He did not like admitting that he was growing old, what with a young wife and four young sons. It seemed a pity he would not be able to enjoy them as he had taken pleasure from his other four children when they were small.

"Mr. Collier, I'm pleased to meet you," Peter said, extending a greeting.

John took the man's hand and stared deeply into his face as if experiencing a moment of recognition. It was a moment before he shook the hand, but he could not take his gaze from Peter's features. "My pleasure, Mr. Phenwick."

"I d'clare, you're staring at Mr. Phenwick like you recognized him from someplace," Nancy interjected.

"He reminds me of someone," John said. "There's a certain familiarity about him."

"If you were to meet my son Joshua, I'm told there is a strong resemblance," Peter commented with a broad smile. "If you can imagine how Stuart will look in forty years; now you can see a similarity to my youth. You no doubt are seeing that Phenwick expression that Stuart possesses, those handsome good looks, the erect posture and the eyes that flash through you. Those were mine when I was younger. Very much like my father and my half brother, Elias."

"Your father? Danny?" John questioned.

"That was what my father was called," Peter returned with a brief chuckle. "I see you've heard about him."

"Yes," John replied quickly, glancing toward Stuart. "Your grandson told me about him."

"Ah, that's the case," Peter said. "I'm certain he didn't tell you everything about my poor father. The man lived a somewhat tormented existence. Alas, that is neither here nor there, and nothing about which any of us can do. He has gone beyond, of course, many years ago. I trust he is less troubled than he was in the past."

"I d'clare, Mr. Phenwick, you never told me your father was a troubled man," Nancy mentioned.

Why did Peter Phenwick look so familiar to John? He could not believe it was simply a resemblance to Stuart. Something else about Peter bothered the young man, that distant familiarity. His personality was one he seemed to recall from somewhere, but where?

The evening proceeded as expected. Joyously happy. The longer it went on the more Nancy and Peter Phenwick came to feel close to John Collier. Peter had also felt an awareness about the youth that made him not a stranger. He wondered about that, for Peter was not a man who made rapid friendships.

On the following Saturday, Nancy made arrangements for John Collier to go to Phenwick House to meet her dear friend Marcia. Sparkling dark-haired beauty that she was, Marcia instantly dazzled the man. Her charm and personality were so warm and outgoing, and her enthusiasm for life so overflowing, that John immediately experienced a friendly rapport. He did not have the sensation with her that he had had with Peter Phenwick, that distant familiarity was not there.

"So you are the young friend that Stuart has been going on about," Marcia exclaimed, her voice music as she spoke.

"I'm his friend. I don't know what sort of nonsense Stuart has been going on about," John replied. "He is a wonderful person. And I am grateful to him for more than words can express."

"I know Stuart quite well," Marcia said. "We have been close for many years. I'll be perfectly honest with you—I've never seen him such an altered person as he has been since you have been staying with him. It's strange he didn't speak of you in the past."

"In the past? We had only met that time in Savannah," John said honestly.

"Only met. Stuart gave me the impression that he had known you for years. Perhaps that was merely my interpretation." Marcia always smiled sweetly, not betraying any feelings that might be beneath her lovely expression.

"I'm certain he has no reason to deceive you as far as I'm concerned," John stated. "We all interpret things as we want to, don't we?"

"I didn't mean to imply deception of any kind," Marcia commented. She smoothed her dress. "Stuart tells me you have an interest in my grandmother."

"If your grandmother is Patricia Phenwick, I do."

"What *is* your interest?"

"A few years ago when I was traveling about, I met a man by the name of Clarence Hoskins who said he once worked for your grandmother. He was a kind of self-styled detective. I would just like to meet her, that is all."

"I'm certain that can be arranged when she's feeling a little better," Marcia assured him. "She's not up to her old self today. We don't want to disturb. Besides I wanted to meet you first, to get to know you. I will relay to Grandma*ma* what you are like. It is her way of testing me to see if I am a good judge of character."

"Do you think I am a respectable character, Miss Phenwick?"

"I would say you were more than respectable, Mr. Collier," Marcia returned pleasantly. "You seem to be a gentleman of the finest kind. You appear to have a command of yourself. Are you at all interested in the arts?"

"No, I can't say that I am," John replied. "Except I have an appreciation for beauty."

"That's a pity. Grandma*ma* likes artists. She has always kept a retinue of dashing young men about her. Not that I was suggesting you become part of that entourage. They've more or less gone their own ways as far as Grandma*ma* is concerned. I still hold salons here at Edward House. I have my friends, many of whom are hers. She no longer takes the interest she did when she was younger. She's exceptionally up in years and has a longing to be younger than she is. Growing old was not her idea at all. It just happened. The realization has upset her."

"Upset her?"

"She was a woman who always delighted in a youthful appearance," Marcia explained. "When age came to her it arrived as a distinct shock. She wasn't ready to accept it. There was an illness when she was in her seventies that weakened her. From that time on, she has progressively become more disabled. It bothers her, that is all."

John's attention was attracted to a painting at the side of the room which was still placed on an easel. He strained to see the likeness.

"Would you like to examine that, Mr. Collier?" Marcia asked.

"Is it by one of your artist friends?"

"It is," Marcia replied. "It's still unfinished. The subject has been done, but the background is still to be completed by Raymond Nelson, the artist. He started it last autumn. It is such a lovely likeness of Kate that we leave it there."

"Kate?" John asked. "I very much would like to see."

He rose and went to the easel, following as near behind Marcia as he could, avoiding her wide skirt.

"She's lovely, isn't she?" Marcia stated. "I believe Raymond has done an admirable job of capturing her likeness. He has painted one of me you must see sometime. It's up in Grandmama's room. She likes to keep it there. This will hang in the same room once it's finished. For now it remains in the parlor. Grandmama doesn't often leave her suite of rooms these days."

"Such a fragile beauty, not quite like—" John caught himself.

"Not like mine? Is that what you were going to say, Mr. Collier?" Marcia questioned.

"I don't believe I was," he stammered. "I can see there's a family resemblance, but—"

"You shouldn't see a family resemblance at all, Mr. Collier. Kate is my cousin only because I was adopted into the Phenwick family. We are not really related at all."

"Oh." He was absorbed in the painting. "Such remarkable beauty. Not that I don't think your beauty equally remarkable. I've never seen so many lovely ladies in my life as are in the Phenwick family."

"Kate Phenwick will be at the wedding. You will meet her then. Perhaps she and Rebecca will come early, since Kate will be my maid of honor."

"I should like very much to meet her," John said. "I confess I am quite attracted to the portrait. If the likeness is anything like the lady, I'm certain to be overwhelmed."

"You are a gallant gentleman, aren't you?" Marcia commented, laughing lightly as she moved back across the room, her skirts rustling as she went. "You and Kate might get along quite well."

Marcia sat as she watched the man appraising the portrait. He was staring intently, almost hypnotized by the likeness therein. At the same time she was appraising him as a man. What she saw fascinated her. Something extremely sensual about him, she thought, something appealing, masculine, yet very genteel. It was the way she used to look at men before she made up her mind to marry Stuart Phenwick, before she realized she was deeply in love. It was in moments like this when she was in the presence of other men that the question began to raise itself in her mind. She had difficulty erasing shadows of doubt that presented themselves. He was indeed handsome, in her opinion, a man who could easily win a woman's heart. She was surprised he had neglected that part of his life. Yet she knew how adventurers were, men of the sea. Was he a man who could be relied upon? Trusted? From all indications she had no reason even to broach the question. Or was there something deceptive about him? Chances are he was not. And what was that quality that had attracted her husband-to-be to him? That was the most perplexing question of all. There had never been any other women with Stuart. Why should she feel that his friendship with this man might pose some kind of threat to her?

Impossible thoughts! Marcia put them from her mind.

"You will come again next week to visit, won't you, Mr. Collier?" Marcia questioned as she saw him to the door. "If you can get away from Medallion long enough some morning, I am certain Grandma*ma* will feel strong enough to meet you."

"I will have to speak with Stuart about that."

"I will make the arrangements," Marcia said assuredly. She leaned against the door and stared again at the man. "What is your precise relationship to Stuart Phenwick, Mr. Collier?"

The question disturbed him because he sensed a tension behind her words. "He is my friend. As I trust you will be."

"Do you? Why?"

"Because I like you very much," John replied simply.

"I hope the three of us will be equally good friends. Certainly Stuart's wife should be—"

"Should be?" Marcia cocked an eyebrow. "Mr. Collier, I believe you are an honest, sincere young man. I want to trust in you. I pray you will never give me opportunity to feel that I have misplaced that trust. Do you understand what I mean?"

"I'm afraid I don't," he said, blushing and covering with a light chuckle. "One day, when I marry, I would like the four of us to be close. I am not experienced with women in an emotional sense. I confess I would like to know I had a friend like you with whom I could discuss such things."

"You've never been with a woman?" Marcia questioned.

"That is a personal question, Miss Phenwick," John replied. "I have had occasional experiences with ladies while I was in the company of Clarence Hoskins—none of which I am particularly proud of. Perhaps that is a blot on my reputation. I trust it will not be. A man must have certain experiences. That is what Clarence told me. I do not make a practice of doing such things. Fact is, that was a year or so back, once in St. Louis and twice in New Orleans. I am perfectly honest about it. And I will be honest with my—that is—when I marry. Does that answer your question?"

A smile came to Marcia's lovely lips. She raised forward on tiptoes and kissed him gently on the cheek. "I like you, John Collier. And I know we shall become good friends. You understand I wanted to know the kind of associate Stuart had taken as a comrade. That's understandable, isn't it?"

"I have no intention of leading him astray as Clarence—"

"I never suspected that you might, John." She kissed him again and shook his hand. "Good day. I think next

180

Wednesday would be a fine time to come and visit. You will plan to stay and have lunch with me."

John left the large door, hesitatingly going down the steps. He turned back for one last picture of the beautiful lady before he practically danced down the street toward the house where he was staying.

# CHAPTER SIXTEEN

Arrangements had been made. The following Wednesday morning, John appeared at Edward House precisely at ten o'clock. He was well dressed in a blue suit, which accentuated his physical coloring and handsomeness. At Stuart's urging, John had disposed of his old clothing and was progressively gathering a fine wardrobe. He presented an impressive picture.

John was let in by the servant, who suggested he wait in the entrance hall until Miss Marcia was prepared to join him. A bench was provided in that impressively ornate foyer. He stared up the stairs leading to the second floor, at the paintings, the polished woodwork, the carpet with the oriental design. While the furnishings themselves were not particularly familiar to the youth, the general atmosphere was. Why did the name Barrywell come to his mind? Barrywell?

John rose and went to the banister, turning around so

that he was facing the door. "To the right are the double doors leading to the ballroom," he thought, "and to the left is the door going to the library." Had someone told him that? The parlor and dining room were in the back of the house, overlooking the garden. Of course he had been in the parlor on his last visit. But he had been taken directly to that room. All the other doors had been closed. He tried to remember if mention had been made of the other rooms.

Going to his right, he cracked the door and discovered it did indeed lead to a room large enough to be a ballroom. His reflection was caught in the many mirrors about the room. Curiously he entered. Morning sun brightened the room. A beam of light seemed to fall directly on the face of the enormous painting at the far end of the space. He went toward it, but stopped a little beyond the center of the room.

"Augusta Phenwick," he exclaimed as he stared at the awesome portrait. How did he know that that particular painting was of Augusta? Why did he not think it to be Patricia or one of the other Phenwick ancestors? He felt absolutely certain of the identity; a fact that caused him to shudder.

Fascination caused him to move nearer. "So we meet again," he commented without thinking. Then, "I mean, *at last* we meet, Augusta Phenwick." He was inundated with a terrible awareness of the fragrance of violets, which caused him to sneeze. Did he hear faint laughter as he did so? Impossible! Backing away, he stared incredulously at the likeness of the first Phenwick woman as if he expected her any moment to leap from the painting and come waltzing toward him.

John was wiping his nose with a handkerchief as he left the ballroom; the seizure of sneezing had caused his eyes to water and his nasal passages to drip. Quickly he closed the door behind him.

Staring through hazy eyes at the doorway opposite, John had to know if he was correct about it leading to the library. Again the name Barrywell came to him. He went toward the door, pushed it open and peered in. No mistaking the fact that the shelf-lined room was a library. More portraits and row upon row of neatly arranged books.

Were his eyes still teary from his bout with sneezing, or had they suddenly clouded more as he gazed at the picture of the handsome young man? Danny. He went nearer. The pose of Daniel Phenwick had been captured when he was in his late teens. Boyish innocence was beautifully captured. Reddish-blond hair glistened, lavender-blue eyes had an abstract sparkle. The features were finely molded and unbelievably handsome. When he read the artist's signature, an image of a thin, wiry person came to his mind. He instinctively knew that Clayton Latshaw must have been a loving man, devoted to the subject of his painting.

As John gazed at the portrait, he had the feeling that his vision was moving deeply into and perhaps seeing through it. There was an old stable with a room above it which had been made into an artist's studio. Three boys were posing for a sketch by the same wiry man he had identified with the name of Clayton Latshaw. The scene changed and the three boys were romping on the summer beach, naked in the sun. The artist was there, sketching them at play. One by one the boys posed for him and a quick rendering was made. The boys appeared to have a remarkable closeness with each other and a fond affection for the man who was their mentor.

The pictures in John's mind changed again. This time there was a solitary boy, the least handsome of the lot.

He was sitting for Clayton Latshaw in his studio. Tears streaked down the youthful face and twice he broke into severe sobbing. Before his mind's eye, that boy grew older, into his teens and early manhood. The tears did not disappear.

A desperate feeling of melancholia came over John. He closed his eyes but the pictures would not disappear. It was all he could do to contain tears himself.

"Ah, here you are, John Collier!" Marcia stated as she appeared at the door. She was wearing a lightweight spring dress, pale blue and smartly attractive. Her almost raven black hair had a free flow to it and a darker blue ribbon was around it. She held her full skirts as she seemed to waft into the room.

John's eyes blinked open. Fear, as a child might have when caught doing something he should not. Pivoting, he identified the intruder and forced a sneeze as an excuse to use his handkerchief to wipe his nose and eyes. "Miss Phenwick! I hope you will not think I was prying by letting myself into this room. The bench is not the most comfortable upon which I have sat. Besides I had a restless curiosity."

"This is a pleasant room for a chat," Marcia said, going to him and offering her cheek for a kiss. Awkwardly he responded. "Do you have hay fever? This is the time of year for it with all the pollen in the air. Come have a seat."

"I must say you look gloriously lovely today, Miss Phenwick," John said stiffly.

"Loveliness is a reflection in the eye of the beholder," Marcia said, positioning herself in a comfortable chair and indicating one opposite for John.

"My eyesight has never been that superior," John returned.

"You do know how to flatter a lady, don't you?"

"Not idle flattery, Miss Marcia."

"Whatever it is, I appreciate it," Marcia remarked. "You were studying the likeness of Daniel Phenwick?"

"Is that a picture of Danny?"

"Danny? You speak as if you know him."

John blushed. "I can see a stark resemblance to Stuart in his great-grandfather's face. And I can see a likeness to Stuart's grandfather as well."

"Is that all you saw in the picture?" Marcia asked.

Could she read his mind? "What more is there?" John felt uneasy. "I was thinking what a fleeting thing youth is. The man in the portrait had grown old, the body died and was buried. Still that moment in time was captured by Clayton Latshaw—I read the artist's signature."

"You are philosophical this morning, aren't you?"

"Looking at something as lasting as that likeness gives me cause to meditate, Miss Marcia."

"What a deep young man you must be," she commented, now studying his face. "Depth of mind and depth of character."

"It is kind of you to say that."

"Not kindness, simple truth," Marcia said. Her eyes were now wandering over the man with a remarkable fascination.

"Spending so much time at sea, and reading so many romantic novels," John stated, "makes a person somewhat of an idealistic dreamer. Even when I was a boy back on the farm, I used to find myself absorbed in deep contemplation. My sister Nellie said I had a dreamy nature. She encouraged me to leave home. She is very intuitive."

"You were raised on a farm?" questioned Marcia. "Yet you speak and have the manners of a gentleman."

"I learned to be what I am," John returned.

"Stuart came to see me last evening," Marcia related,

187

changing the subject. "I must say he certainly speaks in glowing terms about you."

"I don't have the poetic facility to reveal the phrases he uses to express your beauty and the beautiful love he has for you," John stated. "Can you imagine? He actually asked me to be his best man."

"What better choice," Marcia asked, "since you are his good friend?"

"I would think that honor would go to his brother," John said. "After all, it is a matter of family tradition, isn't it?"

"Not necessarily. One should not feel obligated about such things," Marcia commented. "Besides, Gordon Phenwick is not one of my favorite persons. I don't like his pious attitude or the way he attempts to convert people to his way of thinking. A man should be free to think as he likes, I don't deny him that, but Gordon believes he has the right to force himself on one and all. I find him a tremendous bore."

A burst of energy came bubbling into the room. It was Jane Augusta, dressed in yellow and looking as happy as a daffodil. "Excuse me for interrupting."

"Jane Augusta, come in," Marcia bade. "Do you know Mr. John Collier?"

"I don't believe I've had the pleasure," Jane Augusta said, going toward the man.

John was on his feet, uncertain what sort of greeting he should extend to this lady.

"This is Cousin Jane Augusta Clark," Marcia introduced.

"Jane Augusta Ornby-Clark," Jane Augusta corrected. "I'm proud of the fact that I'm an Ornby. I'm actually a Phenwick once removed. I think that is the proper way of expressing it." She curtsied somewhat awkwardly to the man.

"My pleasure, Mrs. Ornby-Clark," John recited.

"My goodness, call me Cousin Jane Augusta," the jolly older woman stated. "Everybody does—even those who aren't related to me." She giggled. The presence of a handsome young man caused her to have a reaction, too.

"Cousin Jane Augusta it will be," John said brightly, a smile welcoming the friendship.

"Cousin Jane Augusta comes regularly to look in on Grandmama," Marcia informed him. "She's very devoted."

"I'm a widow lady myself," Jane Augusta said. "I have plenty of time. Besides I am dearly fond of Aunt Patricia—and of Marcia. Forgive me if I'm interfering with your chat. Aunt Patricia sent me down to inform that she is ready to meet Mr. Collier."

"Jane Augusta? Then you must have been named for the lady in the portrait that hangs in the ballroom," John stated.

"Named for my own grandmother, Jane, and my great-grandmother, Augusta," Jane Augusta explained. "I'm the eldest of several children. Only my brothers Theodore and Daniel live in Boston now. The others have gone to other places. I don't always keep close contact with them. They have their lives. Besides, I have my hands full with my brothers and their families, and all the Phenwick cousins and kin." She bubbled laughter. "Do you have family here in Boston, John?"

"No. My family live far to the west of here," John returned. "I was just speaking of my sister Nellie. Now that I think of it, she would be very out of place in Boston."

"John was raised on a farm, weren't you?" Marcia said.

"How very interesting," Jane Augusta gushed. "I have a little garden of my own. Members of my family get after me for puttering about raising vegetables. They think it's undignified for a lady of my age and position. But I assure them I am perfectly happy working in the soil. It gives me an earthy feeling, if you know what I mean."

John knew. "I don't think I'll ever get the Illinois dirt completely from under my fingernails."

"They look spotlessly clean to me," Jane Augusta returned. "Oh, I see what you mean—I think. I don't have a very sophisticated sense of humor. Forgive me, John."

"There's nothing to forgive. I'm a self-educated country boy who has pulled himself up by the bootstraps. Now I am intruding upon the Phenwicks."

"Not intruding, John," Marcia assured him. "Your presence is well appreciated. The final test of approval lies with Grandma*ma*. Shall we go have a visit?"

John tried to swallow the lump that had come to his throat. It was difficult.

# CHAPTER SEVENTEEN

"Time is an elegant mask-maker," Patricia Phenwick remarked as she sat in her thronelike chair. The meticulously neat room was splendid with fine furnishings. The portrait of Marcia was prominent, as were the likenesses of Edward and Elias Phenwick, the lady's two late husbands. "So you are the notorious John Collier of whom I've heard. Please sit, Mr. Collier. Even these old tired eyes are impressed with your comely figure and features. I have always been a connoisseur of glorious young men. My past is jaded with delicious memories. But what is life for if it's not to enjoy?"

"You sound to be a very worldly woman, Mrs. Phenwick," John commented.

"I certainly hope so. I wouldn't want it any other way," Patricia returned. "But there comes a time when one lives with luscious memories alone and no longer experiences the delight of creating new and exciting innovation. Do I strike you as being bizarre, Mr. Collier?"

"Most unusual."

"I'm pleased. The thought of becoming mundane with age appalls me. Yet some things are inevitable." Patricia chuckled. "There are men and there are men, Mr. Collier. I don't disturb you by discussing such matters, do I?"

"No."

"Many of my artistic friends, the lithe men with varying degrees of talent, are a vivid contrast to the more solidly masculine types," Patricia continued. "I don't see much if any of the artist in you, Mr. Collier. But I do behold a handsome gentleman who no doubt has broken many a heart."

John blushed. "None that I know of, Mrs. Phenwick. I've spent a good deal of time traveling and at sea, except when I was a boy back on the farm."

"I would have never taken you for a farm boy. Yet I can see you are sturdily constructed, an indication of considerable physical labor. And a seaman, too? My mind is a scrapbook of memories when it comes to that topic."

"When I was in Quincy, Illinois," John informed her, feeling slightly uncomfortable at the trend of the conversation, "I met a fellow by the name of Clarence Hospins. He said he once worked for you."

"Clarence Hoskins?" Patricia looked perplexed.

"Wasn't that the man you hired down in Savannah to protect Harriet Cox before she married Prentise?" asked Jane Augusta, who had a remarkable memory for names at times.

"Hoskins? Savannah?" A dim smile came to Patricia's lips. "Oh yes. Clarence. I knew your friend intimately well, Mr. Collier—for a short period of time. I rather liked him because he was the antithesis of my artistic young men. I appreciate a man who has a basic quality."

"He was the one who led John into romantic encounters," Marcia inserted.

"Did he? Really?" Patricia smirked. "I've no doubt he would be a good instructor."

John had become a fiery red. "He only—that is—he—"

"Don't explain, Mr. Collier," Patricia interrupted. "Let my own mind weave in the details. And my dear Marcia, you have embarrassed our guest."

"I'm not—that is—maybe I am."

Jane Augusta giggled, holding her hand to her mouth.

"I have long been of the opinion," Patricia said, taking the conversation again, "that a man should be experienced in matters of expressing himself, while a young lady should maintain an innocent facade for as long as it is humanly possible. It makes it terribly awkward when both man and woman are inexperienced. Instinct is one thing, skill is another."

"Grandma*ma*!"

"In every aspect of life, Marcia," Patricia stated, not to be reprimanded for her words. "And what is your opinion, Mr. Collier, of my nephew, Stuart?"

"Stuart is a fine person, a good friend," John managed to reply, still attempting to overcome his self-consciousness. "I could ask for no finer companion."

"You have moved into Augustus' old house with him, haven't you?"

"I have Gordon's room. It is more than sufficient to my needs."

"I have spoken with Stuart," Patricia said. "I must say you have brought a noticeable change to the lad. I've often felt a little sorry for the boy. I, as was Jane Augusta, was with him at the time his mother was killed in that terrible fire. I feel no pity for her death, only for her confused state of mind. Stuart was deeply affected by that incident. His mother had discouraged his friendship with other youths of his age. I can well see how he would latch on to a friendship such as yours. Are you a moral man, Mr. Collier?"

"I believe I am. I have high ideals and principles. While I'm not affiliated with a church, I try to live a righteous life," John replied. "Is that what you mean?"

"It comes close," Patricia remarked. "Marcia tells me you were impressed with the likeness of my granddaughter, Kate Phenwick Cathcart."

"Grandma*ma*, you shouldn't—"

"Tut-tut, Marcia, I am still the matriarch of this family," Patricia announced. "Is that not true, Mr. Collier?"

"You mean about the painting?"

"Yes."

"I found her pleasant and appealing."

"A good answer."

John sneezed. "Excuse me. I'm sorry."

"Bless you, John Collier," Patricia commented.

"I suspect John has hay fever," Marcia said.

John put his handkerchief to his nose. "No, it was the scent of—" He stopped, feeling suddenly uncomfortable under the penetrating stares of the three ladies.

"The scent of what, Mr. Collier?" asked Patricia.

He looked about the room. No fresh flowers. "Of some kind of flower."

"What kind precisely, Mr. Collier?" Patricia probed. "Surely you must know if a particular flower makes you sneeze."

"Yes . . ." Again he looked around. "Violets."

A broad smile came to the old lady's face. "Violets when you were speaking of the likeness of Kate? I rather had a premonition it was violets." Then realizing the youth's embarrassment, she said, "I believe I have a violet-scented sachet somewhere. I confess I don't recall where it is, or I would have it removed so it does not disturb you again."

"I didn't know you had a violet sachet, Aunt Patricia," Jane Augusta interjected.

"There are many things you don't know about me, Jane Augusta," the old woman said. She turned her attention again to John.

The servant appeared to announce the arrival of Dr. Theodore Ornby.

"Ted is early. Or perhaps it is later than I imagine," Patricia stated. "Well, well, we will have to continue this little interview at another time, John Collier. Will you come and have tea with me one day? Sometime next week, if it pleases you."

"I would be honored, Mrs. Phenwick."

Theodore Ornby ambled casually into the room. He acknowledged the presence of the ladies and was properly introduced to John Collier.

"A pleasure, Mr. Collier, I'm sure," Dr. Ted said. "So you're the young man who has taken up with Cousin Stuart, are you?"

"Stuart is my friend."

"Mr. Collier has a remarkable problem of sneezing when in the presence of violets, Ted," Patricia related. "Perhaps it is a situation you can help him with. Might I suggest that he wait to chat with you in the library?"

"I have a relaxed schedule today," Dr. Ted returned. "Certainly I will have time for a chat with the young man. Now, if I'm not too greatly disturbing you, Aunt Patricia, I think I had better have a feel of the pulse and a listen or two."

"It's time for me to be prodded and thumped," Patricia said. "You will excuse me—both of you. Jane Augusta may stay."

John bowed as he said goodbye to Patricia. Marcia accompanied him from the room with the promise she would show him to the library.

"What are you being so mysterious about, Aunt?" asked Dr. Ted after he had examined the old lady.

"Who is being mysterious?"

"You. Your pulse is up. That means either that you had a difficult night or that you're excited about some scheme that is rattling around in that brain of yours," Dr. Ted replied.

"You know me too well, Ted."

"I've been your physician too long not to be aware of your moods," Ted said, closing his medical bag. "What is it?"

"Ted, you know I've never been a great believer in fate," Patricia related, "because the individual has a certain control over his destiny. But I do believe there are invisible forces around who somehow have a way of making circumstances come together."

"An interesting statement, Aunt Patricia. What are you getting at?"

"Yes, Aunt Patricia," chimed Jane Augusta.

"For close to a century, this family has been concerned about the Phenwick women," Patricia said with a quiet smile. "That was dear Augusta's doing. Now I'm beginning to wonder if she hasn't taken a hand in selecting Phenwick men as well."

"What sort of nonsense—?"

"Not nonsense, Ted, merely a hypothesis. For instance, I'm convinced that both Marcia and her brother, Gregory, became Phenwicks through the old girl's intervention," Patricia continued. "Gregory is now a Phenwick man. On that premise, could it not be that others—

say Robert Cathcart, for instance—were directed to a Phenwick woman by that invisible force?"

"Aunt Patricia—"

"I know. You think I'm getting balmy in my old age, don't you? Never mind. Jane Augusta, let me assure you I have never owned a violet sachet in my life. But you will attest to the fact that John Collier reacted to the scent of violets with a remarkable burst of sneezing. Isn't that true?"

"Oh, he very definitely sneezed," Jane Augusta said.

"Then he has a sinus problem," Ted stated.

"There is less of the romantic in you than I thought, Ted," Patricia commented. "Very well, suppose it is just fantasy that I believe Augusta makes her presence—and her approval—known with the scent of violets. I have no physical proof to argue that point. Jane Augusta, tell your brother that John Collier decidedly said it was the fragrance of violets that made him sneeze."

"Oh, it was, Teddy."

"Which has to do with what?" Ted questioned, enjoying the game.

"Let us go back to a conversation we had some time back, Ted," Patricia said. "When we were discussing Kate Phenwick, my granddaughter. You made a statement that you believed she could well be the reincarnation of Danny."

"It wasn't so much a statement, Aunt, as it was a suggestion," Ted corrected. "We can't be certain of those things."

"Very well. And you also suggested that Rebecca could be the reembodiment of Rachel, which would explain the fanatical love both Elias, her father, and Johnny Ornby, her husband, had for her. They were both uncontrollably in love with Rachel. I certainly was aware that Rebecca was always Elias' daughter . . . only mine through circumstance. If we go along with the reincarnationist theory—I confess I'm still skeptical—there is a kind of missing link. I come to the name of Michael O'Plaggerty."

"Michael O'Plaggerty?" Ted sat forward.

"I recall Edward telling me of Michael and the adventures they shared together with Danny when they were children," Patricia related. "Danny had a strange closeness to Edward and became very dependent upon him until Edward joined the army. Up until that time Michael had been in the background, since he was the son of an indentured slave and Augusta had chosen to adopt Edward along with Jane as Phenwick children. When Danny was in the army and became lost in battle, or whatever happened to him, it was Michael, not Edward, who went out searching for him. By the time Michael returned to Greenfield, Danny's children had all been born, but he was not a good father. As you know, Elias, his eldest, accidentally was by some woman of the neighborhood, not born to Margaret. When a scandal was about to erupt over that, Michael made arrangements and adopted Elias as his own son. It wasn't until years later that Danny discovered that he was Elias' father and took legal means to make amends for his neglect."

"I didn't know all of this, Aunt Patricia," Jane said.

"Well, you're learning about it now. Maybe you'd better write it down somewhere so it will be on record," Patricia suggested. "But I've gotten ahead of myself. You see, it was Michael who desperately tried to help Rachel when she first began having problems. He was attacked by her, but somehow managed to sustain love and compassion for her. Michael O'Plaggerty. Remember that name. I have an intuition."

"About Michael O'Plaggerty?" questioned Jane Augusta. "Surely he's dead by now."

"He is . . . or at least he was."

"*Was?*" Ted twitched. He was jumping ahead of his aunt's thoughts.

"We cannot know how much Michael did for Danny up until the end," Patricia stated. "Jane told me he took care of Danny in those years he returned to Greenfield, but refused to stay in Phenwick House. That kind of devotion of one person for another is a beauty unto itself. I wonder if Danny and Michael weren't somehow soul mates. According to Rosea Hackleby, soul mates didn't always appear in the physical as lovers or even as being closely related through blood lines. Yet, hypothetically again, if an entity had associated in a situation such as that with Danny and Michael, might he not repeat a smiliar pattern for a while in a following life?"

"I don't understand you at all," Jane Augusta said.

"I think I'm beginning to realize what you're getting at, Aunt Patricia," Ted commented, rising from where he had been sitting. "I almost forgot about that young man waiting to see me in the library. I would like to hear your further theories, Aunt Patricia."

"I think you have gotten the gist of what I was trying to say, Ted. Go have a chat with John Collier."

# CHAPTER EIGHTEEN

"Grandma*ma*, Dr. Ted said you wished to see me."
Marcia returned to the suite of rooms on the second
floor.

"I have made a decision," Patricia informed her. "I
want you to sit and write a letter to Rebecca and Kate,
inviting them to come as soon as possible to Boston."

"The wedding isn't until the latter part of June," Jane
Augusta inserted. "Besides, I could have written the letter for you, Aunt Patricia."

"Thank you anyway, Jane Augusta," Patricia remarked. "The letter should come from Marcia. She is the
bride-to-be."

"I'll write whatever you wish, Grandma*ma*," Marcia
stated, going to the writing desk and finding paper. "I
confess I don't understand the urgency."

"It will be nearly the end of May before they can get
here," Patricia returned. "That's hardly enough time for

all the preparation. Besides, I want Rebecca near me for a while. We have not been close as mother and daughter, not as we should have been. I feel Susannah and I became closer while she was with me the last time. Susannah and Gregory will be here by the middle of June, and I trust Jim Cornhill. I would like all of us to be together in the same house for a few weeks. Perhaps I'm merely being sentimental."

"You? Sentimental, Aunt Patricia?" Jane Augusta asked.

"My dear Jane Augusta, you might be surprised at your old Aunt Patricia. One cannot have a highly romantic nature without being sentimental once in a while. Before I breathe my last in this life, I should really set down my version of the Phenwick history—or have one of you write it for me."

"I would love to do that," Marcia volunteered. "I have often thought about it."

"Then we really must get to it as soon after the wedding as you've gathered your senses and come back to earth," Patricia said lightly. "Now address the letter to both Rebecca and Kate."

After informing Marcia that Patricia would like to see her again, Dr. Ted walked with her to the foot of the stairs. It was a ploy to leave John Collier alone in the library for a few moments. When the doctor returned, he was not surprised to find the young man gazing at the portrait of Danny.

"Now then, John Collier."

"Have you returned so soon, Dr. Ornby?"

"Let's dispense with the Ornby part and just call me Dr. Ted. I really have to stop and think who Dr. Ornby is, I've been called the other for so long." Ted chuckled. "Familiarity does not necessarily lessen respect. Fact is, I find I have an easier working arrangement with my patients when things are handled in a less formal way." He went to the painting. "A beautiful piece of artwork, isn't it? I've always liked that particular painting."

"Yes, I was admiring it," John said, feeling a bit uneasy. "I am curious to know about what you wanted to chat with me, Dr. Ted."

"All things in due time, my boy," Dr. Ted said, putting his arm to John's shoulder. "It seems to me you have a singular reaction to that portrait. Is there a reason?"

"I find it interesting," John replied.

"Are you often attracted to the comeliness of men?" Dr. Ted bluntly asked.

"I don't know what you mean."

"I have become aware through my studies," Dr. Ted related in a clinical way, "that there are those men who are physically drawn to other men, emotionally and sensually. It is certainly not a matter that is publicized, but a situation that has been whispered about behind fans and through gusts of cigar smoke. Nothing mentioned in polite conversation. You'll forgive me, then, if I seem impolite for a moment."

John registered an expression of utter shock. "Good heavens! You're not suggesting that because I—that is—I find this likeness intriguing that I— Oh no! That's *not* the case with me, I assure you."

"I only asked out of curiosity," Dr. Ted said, "especially since you have developed such a remarkable friendship with my cousin. I have spoken with him indirectly about the matter, and I confess he projects an attitude of complete innocence. I have not been quite so blunt with him."

"I should hope not." John showed extreme annoyance.

"If there is any such speculation, I will instantly move from his home. We are friends."

"Platonic friends?"

John had to think of the word. "Yes, strictly platonic. I never dreamed—"

"Enough. We'll drop the matter. You have clarified any doubt that could have possibly been in my mind," Ted assured him. "As a physician and a man interested in the psychological nature of individuals, I'm afraid I have a very straightforward approach . . . that is, in most cases. Why don't we go into the parlor where the seats are more comfortable and we can gaze out at Aunt Patricia's lovely spring garden? There's a door right here that leads directly to it."

John was noticeably shaken. The idea projected by Dr. Ted had appalled him. Obediently he followed the doctor's direction.

"Ah yes, this is much better," Dr. Ted said, stretching. He went to the window to stare at the explosion of lilacs outside.

John hesitated at the painting of Kate.

"Do you like flowers, John?"

"I beg your pardon." John looked up from the painting.

"Oh, I'm sorry," Ted returned when he realized that the youth was preoccupied. "Lovely, isn't she?"

"Marcia told me it is Kate Phenwick," John remarked, forcing his glance away from the portrait. "The artist still has to finish the background."

Ted took a seat on the opposite side of the room. "Lovely Kate was here in Boston last autumn. She'll be returning again for the wedding."

John moved to a chair opposite the doctor. "You asked me if I liked violets?"

"No." Dr. Ted chuckled. "I asked if you liked lilacs."

"I do. My mother used to have four lilac bushes that were her pride, back on the farm," John explained. "While they were in bloom each spring, I remember she would gather bunches of them and put them in a pickle crock on the table. Often she would go smell them. Funny, I haven't thought of that in a long time."

"You are fond of your mother?"

"She's a good woman, good to all her children," John declared. "But when the time came, like a mother robin, she pushed her chicks from the nest and made them fly on their own. I've never been home since I left. But I'd like to go back one day."

"Strange you mentioned violets while looking at Kate's likeness."

"Did I mention—? Oh yes, I thought you had said violets."

"Or perhaps they were on your mind."

John said, "Violets make me sneeze."

"Why?"

"What? I don't know. They just always have."

"Even when violets aren't anywhere around."

"Oh, Mrs. Phenwick told you—but she said she had sachet someplace in the room."

"Some things that make us have peculiar reactions are largely in our minds," Ted stated. "I used to have a patient who complained of pain in his ankle whenever the word 'dog' was mentioned. Well, it turned out he had been bitten by a dog on his ankle when he was a boy. Once he recalled that and knew it was a reaction from the past, he didn't have any more pains when dogs were mentioned."

"Are you suggesting I might have been bitten by a violet?"

Ted laughed. "I like your sense of humor, John. Very amusing. I can see you are quick-witted. Well, no, I don't believe you had that kind of an encounter with violets, but you might have had some other. When you first walked into this house, did you have the sensation that it was familiar to you?"

"How did you—?" John caught himself and laughed. "Well, I confess Barrywell House seemed vaguely—"

"Barrywell House?" Dr. Ted tapped his fingers together.

Again John laughed, his face flushed. "Oh. I mean Edward House. I must have been thinking of some other place."

"There was a Barrywell House once, here in Boston," Ted explained. "It was built by Augusta Phenwick. Mysteriously Aunt Patricia had it torn down many years ago and had this one constructed after the same plans. My father told me that Edward House was almost identical to the old house in many ways. He said he believed Aunt Patricia did not like the location of it and wanted to live on Beacon Hill. The mirrors in the ballroom came from the old house. She apparently had it demolished because she didn't want another house identical to hers in the entire city." He chuckled. "That's Aunt Patricia for you."

"Barrywell House was torn down *many* years ago?" John questioned.

"When I was a lad," Ted replied, "or maybe before. I don't recall it." He cleared his throat. "Is the name O'Plaggerty familiar to you?"

"O'Plaggerty?" John's eyes suddenly grew wider.

"Uncle Danny was married to one of the O'Plaggerty girls."

"Titter?"

"Titter?" questioned Ted. "Her name was Margaret."

"But she was called Titter because her youngest brother could not say 'sister,' " John said as a matter of fact.

"How do you know that?"

"I don't know." John felt even more uneasy. "Perhaps I should tell you about what happened to me back in Quincy. You seem to be getting at something, maybe I can help you. I was hypnotized. I think the man who did it was some kind of charlatan; but whatever he did must have made something happen. I don't recall anything other than staring at a crystal bauble. The next thing I knew, I was wide awake, feeling as though I had taken a nap. During the time I was unconscious I was asked several questions. A friend took notes. They say I went back in time over a hundred years."

"Very interesting. Would you care to disclose what information was discovered then?" Ted asked.

John related the data he had from the notes he had memorized.

"Do you presently have a sister named Margaret?" Ted asked at the conclusion of the recitation.

"No. There's Abby, Nellie, Martha and Myrtie," John replied. "I was closest to Nellie."

"Michael O *could* have been Michael O'Plaggerty, isn't that what you're thinking, John?"

"*If* Margaret O'Plaggerty was called Titter."

"Is that why you came to Boston, to find the answer to questions that had been festering in you all this time?"

"I suppose it was the real motivation."

"Or was it to find that mysterious alleged soul mate?"

John squirmed and scratched. "That may be possible."

"Then that portrait you were admiring in the library," Ted continued, "might well have been the Danny from your notes?"

"He seems so very familiar." John had a faraway expression.

"I confess I'm no authority on such things," Ted said, "but there may have been a way that you were able to project your subconscious mind back into time and picked up the situation you related about the Phenwicks of Greenfield. That wouldn't necessarily mean you or your soul had ever been there. I have heard of people who can look both into the past and into the future."

"But why would I have said I was going to find *my* soul mate in this life, that we were to be born into two consecutive lives together?" John argued.

"Ah, then you admit your motive is a search for this so-called soul mate?" Ted stated. "It is important to know what you're doing here."

"Do you think I'm crazy, Doctor?" John asked. "Do you think I'm on a wild chipmunk chase? I haven't even admitted to Stuart my motivation for being in Boston."

"Stuart?" Dr. Ted questioned. "I suppose it has occurred to you that Stuart might be the reincarnation of Danny."

"No. I believe—and I can't tell you why I feel so strongly about this—that my soul mate will appear in the form of a woman in this life."

"Because you want it to," Dr. Ted said. He rose. "I would like you to stop by my office sometime in the near future. I want to check on certain specific matters." He shook the boy's hand. "Shall we go to the door? Can I drop you someplace?"

"I rode on horseback," John returned. "Thank you."

"You will come to see me, won't you?"

"I'll get the address from Stuart."

Again Dr. Ted clasped the youth's hand, putting his other hand to the strong young shoulder. "And, between you and me, I don't really believe you're on a wild chipmunk chase." He laughed and went to his shay.

# CHAPTER NINETEEN

When Marcia's letter arrived in Greenfield, Rebecca was immediately opposed to changing her plans. Kate became so insistent that her mother gave in and they altered their schedule. The trip by carriage to Portland was rough, with roads still muddy. The train ride from Portland to Boston was not the most comfortable they had taken. By the time they had reached their destination, even Rebecca had mustered enthusiasm.

When the meeting finally took place between Patricia and her daughter and granddaughter, it was a happy occasion, although the old woman, lacking strength, alarmed Rebecca. She had not expected to see her so drastically changed since the last time they had been together. While never strongly close to Patricia, she did feel a natural tie. Kate, too, noticed a difference in her grandmother, but she had not known her in the days of her glory as a grand hostess.

Marcia and Kate renewed their friendship, seemingly becoming closer than they had been on Kate's last visit to Boston. Perhaps that was due to Marcia's choice of Kate instead of Nancy as matron of honor. That was part of Patricia's doing. Nancy understood and would be in the wedding party anyway.

The next day after their arrival, Rebecca stated she wanted to go to the business district to do some shopping. Naturally she would have to have better clothing for Boston than what she wore in Greenfield. Since Marcia had to go to the dressmaker, and wanted Kate to be measured, she suggested the three of them ride together. Rebecca preferred her own seamstress, who had made clothing for her over the years, to the man who specialized in wedding and party apparel. Besides, she wanted to be on her own and browse about the city, to see the changes and probably run into an old acquaintance or two. The younger ladies welcomed the opportunity to be alone.

Rebecca found that Boston had changed. So many immigrants had come in that she rarely heard English spoken. Nowhere did she encounter anyone from her past. Still she amused herself going from shop to shop, gawking at the sights and observing the many people who now bustled through the streets.

Rebecca had stopped at a jewelry store, scanning the stones and settings on display, when she became aware of the presence of another individual. Instinctively she knew it was a man and that he was intently watching her. She turned to gaze into the smiling face of John Collier.

"Excuse me," he said. "I was just passing and I thought you looked familiar to me." He doffed his hat.

"I do not live in Boston," Rebecca replied, somewhat uneasy under his penetrating stare. "You're far too

210

young to be anyone from my past. Perhaps I merely look like someone you've known."

"That may well be the case," John returned.

"Still as I look at you—there is a resemblance—ah, but to whom?" She laughed lightly, flipping her hand as if to pass the matter off.

John said, "Rachel?"

"I beg your pardon."

"As I was gazing at you," he replied, "the name 'Rachel' came to mind."

Rebecca turned back to the display window of jewels. Her attention seemed to hold on a large blue sapphire. As she did she saw a man clad in buckskin, ruggedly handsome, appearing in the woods.

*"I'm sorry, I didn't realize anyone was here,"* she heard his voice say as he approached a young girl.

*"Neither did I."*

*"Shall I go away and not disturb you?"* asked he.

*"No. Please stay. My name is Rachel Phenwick."*

*"Rachel Phenwick? Yes, of course, you would have to be a Phenwick. The latest Phenwick woman, I should imagine."*

*"I'm not a woman yet. Who are you?"*

*"My name is O'Plaggerty. Have you ever heard of it?"*

*"I'm an O'Plaggerty on my mother's side."*

*"You're not Titter O'Plaggerty's daughter, are you?"*

*"Yes."*

*He held out his hand. "Pleased to meet you. I'm your Uncle Mike. Michael O'Plaggerty."*

"I hope I haven't distressed you, madam," John said, watching her curious reaction.

Rebecca looked up. "What? Oh no. My name isn't Rachel."

"I didn't suppose it would be. Are you by any chance a Phenwick?" John asked perceptively. "You remind me somewhat of Mrs. Patricia Phenwick."

"You know my mother?" Rebecca questioned. "I don't believe I know you."

"You wouldn't. You live in Greenfield, Maine, don't you?"

"How do you know so much about me?" Rebecca returned.

John explained who he was, that he was living with Stuart Phenwick and that he worked for Medallion Enterprises.

"Could you take a few minutes and have a cup of tea with me, Mrs. Cathcart?" John invited.

"Why, I—yes, I believe that would be refreshing. Down home it's only a short stroll to the village square," Rebecca said, now brightening. "One can do all of one's shopping in a matter of a short while. I've been walking about for nearly two hours, Mr. Collier."

They went to a cozy little tea shop and found an isolated corner.

"I knew you were to arrive soon in Boston," John said. "I've been away for two weeks on business for Stuart. I didn't know you had arrived."

"We only got here yesterday," Rebecca explained. She studied the young man, again hearing the distant: *"Pleased to meet you. I'm your Uncle Mike. Michael O'Plaggerty."*

"Mrs. Phenwick and Jane Augusta have spoken of you," John said. "I've been anxious to meet you."

"You're not from Boston, are you?"

"From Illinois."

"What brings you here?"

"I'm trying to put together the pieces of a puzzle," John replied. "Dr. Ted is helping me."

"Is it a physical puzzle? Or one dealing with your mind?"

"That's the part we're still working on," John said with laughter. "You know, I can't get over how familiar you seem to me."

*"I'm your Uncle Mike."*

A picture of old Michael O'Plaggerty came to her mind as she remembered him when she was a young lady. "I don't suppose you ever had any relatives that lived in Greenfield, did you?"

John blushed. "I'm not certain."

"Perhaps that is why you seem faintly familiar to me," Rebecca stated.

"I hope that I will see more of you while you're visiting, Mrs. Cathcart," John said. "Maybe we can discover where we know each other from."

Rebecca smiled, but made no comment. She felt as if she were trembling, or, if she were not, she should be.

"May I see you back to Edward House, Mrs. Cathcart?" John asked a short while later.

"Thank you, no. I have more shopping to do. I shop best by myself or with Ella Shane—a close friend," Rebecca said, trying not to sound flustered. It had been a long time since a young man had bought her anything—even a cup of tea. "It has been pleasant, Mr. Collier. I'll be looking forward to seeing you again sometime."

"As will I, Mrs. Cathcart." John bowed slightly and waved as she left. Why had he been so greatly impressed by the lady? He would go the next day and have a visit with Dr. Ted. He wanted to have a further talk with the doctor sooner, but business had taken him away from the city. Excited, he wished to relate about his experience of that afternoon and the lady who had so deeply impressed him.

Rebecca could not keep her mind on shopping. She kept thinking of John, his flashing eyes, his handsome appearance. Why was she unable to get a vision of her grandfather's death from her mind? *"My name is Rebecca, not Rachel!"* And why did she recall the pathetically heartbroken old man they all called Uncle Mike who kept a constant vigil at her grandfather's deathbed? Maybe she, too, should have a visit with Ted Ornby.

# CHAPTER TWENTY

Dr. Ted did not set up regular appointments. Patients came when they needed to see him; if they stayed away too long that was their problem. Usually he was never so busy that anyone had a long wait; and if he saw he was going to be longer than usual with a person, he would tell the others to go run an errand and come back at a more convenient time.

John Collier had no wait at all that next afternoon when he bounced into Dr. Ted's office.

"I'd about given up on you, boy," Dr. Ted commented, "until Stuart told me you were out of the city for him."

"I was on my way here yesterday afternoon—a little later than this—when I chanced to meet a most interesting lady quite by accident," John explained.

"A lady? Young or old?" Dr. Ted asked, curiously glancing at him.

"In middle years, I would say," John replied. "We had a cup of tea."

"Ah, the powers of persuasion young men possess," Ted commented. "Were there romantic overtones involved?"

"Not that," John replied. "I was walking down the street, passed a jewelry store, and there she was peering in the window. I knew her. I mean, I felt she was someone I should know."

"Were you another sort of man, I would have a different thought," Ted mumbled. "Go on. She appeared familiar to you?"

"That was the thing about it that fascinated me. While she was an attractive person, she was not an exceptional beauty. And, as I say, she was at least a generation older than I. But, as I'm sitting here, I swear I thought I knew her. Well, I was close. It was Rebecca Cathcart, Mrs. Phenwick's daughter."

Ted leaned forward. "Rebecca? Looked familiar? Ah yes, I can see where you might notice a family characteristic. I visited with Rebecca the other day. She has an expression or two of Aunt Patricia's."

"But I did *not* recognize her as a Phenwick—at least not as a present-day Phenwick," John insisted. "I knew her from sometime before. It was like the feeling I had about Barrywell—I mean, Edward House, or the pictures of Danny and Augusta."

"And Kate?"

"You saw that, did you? Yes, I'm certain I recognized something in that picture," John admitted.

"That's most curious," Dr. Ted stated. "If you had lived a previous life with the Phenwicks, directly or indirectly, I can see where there might be a memory of the pictures of Danny and Augusta, or others who lived in that time. But Kate lives *now*. She wouldn't have maintained her same likeness."

"Neither did Mrs. Phenwick or Mrs. Cathcart," John said, "but I felt as if I recognized them."

"But they were alive, albeit years younger, when Danny was still living, and their personalities were still basically the same," Ted submitted. "I am of the belief we recognize one another as much by our personalities as we do by outer physical characteristics. In the case of the portrait of Kate, you saw her likeness on canvas, without the personality present."

"That would explain my confused reaction," John stated, "and why I was hesitant to admit that I saw a familiarity in the painting."

"You know, young man, I wonder if you're not trying to manufacture something here," Dr. Ted said, his fingertips bouncing together. "In a sense you have picked up a suggestion—perhaps dating back to your hypnotic experience in Quincy, Illinois. The suggestion was planted. Clarence Hoskins, I believe that was his name, had mentioned the Phenwick name. He had known the family and some of its background. I'm not saying you did, but you may have picked up his thought waves concerning them, creating this whole illusion that you once had lived in or around the Phenwick family. I've given this thought."

"I don't see how I could have created—" John murmured.

"You've had what—two or three years since that episode with hypnosis—time enough to create thoughts that you would be attracted to," Dr. Ted explained. "This is a whole new avenue of thought, more philosophical than psychological, in that we create whatever future we want. For example, *if* Clarence Hoskins planted certain ideas in your mind and you reacted to them in your subconscious or unawareness, you could have been drawn to them as if they had established a magnetic field attracting you."

"I swear I don't understand what you're talking about, Dr. Ted," John said, scratching his head. "You left me a way back there."

"I was afraid I might," Dr. Ted commented. "It's all theory, my own device based on reading I've done. Still I believe I know what I mean, I've just got to sort it out and make it logical to someone else. But that is my problem, not yours."

"I wish I understood what you're getting at," John said.

"It isn't important to the moment," Dr. Ted confessed. "Maybe one day we can venture further into it. I'll let you read some of the books on the subject. My son, Augustus, sent me a thin volume recently which he had translated into English. Perhaps someday you will read that." He doubled his chins, scowled and put his fingers to his beard. "When was the first time you heard the expression 'soul mate'?"

"That day in Quincy when Clarence read the notes of what I had said," John replied. "I never before dreamed such a thing existed . . . *if* it does."

"Interestingly, Augustus had written to me last winter about such a theory," Dr. Ted remarked. "If I can possibly make the trip, I would like to go over to London, where Augustus will be attending a lecture series this summer. In light of your case, I would enjoy investigating further. Well, well. What I would like to propose to you is that we make another attempt at trying to hypnotize you. I'm no expert, but I've had some success with it. I would bring in a colleague—perhaps my son Joseph—to witness and record what, if anything, was said. Would you be willing to undergo such an experiment?"

"I believe so," John returned. "Yes. Knowing what I now know, there are certain questions I would suggest that you ask."

"Good. Let me speak with Joe, and we'll set up a time some evening when we will not be disturbed," Dr. Ted said. "Now, I heard my outside door open and close a short while ago. It might be a patient with an important problem. I will send word to you at the Medallion office."

Dr. Ted went to open the door for John. They shook hands and the younger man left. "Ah, Mrs. Cutter, won't you bring Samuel and come in?"

John stood in the outer waiting room for a few moments trying to gather his thoughts. He would have liked to have stayed for a longer discussion with the doctor, but he knew the man's time was valuable. Donning his hat, he barged out into the warm but breezy afternoon.

No more had he lunged through the door than John collided with a lovely young lady carrying a parasol. She fell backward and he caught her before she fell. Her handbag and parasol went flying, especially the parasol, which was caught by the breeze.

Adjusting her bonnet, which had been knocked askew, and gasping with indignation, Kate said, "Quickly get my parasol, you clumsy fool, before it goes into the road! I just purchased it yesterday. Hurry before it escapes!"

John scrambled to get the article, losing his hat in the process and having to run after it. He, too, was annoyed.

"Here's your parasol, lady. You should be more careful when you enter places," he suggested heatedly.

"*I* should be more careful, you dolt?" Kate fired. "You were the one who ran into me."

"I believe it was a mutual attempt," John returned, rage dimming his vision.

"Well, I'll not stand here discussing the matter," Kate said emphatically. "Give me my parasol and be off with you. Were I not a lady, I'd strike you with it." She snatched the object from him. Raising her nose and aloofly turning, she marched into the building.

John dusted off his hat as he thought several unkind things about the person with whom he had collided. It was unlike him to have such opinions about people, but the circumstance was such that he had momentarily lost his composure. If he never laid eyes on the lady again it would be too soon.

A few moments later, as he was striding at a fast gait down the street, he had another thought and said aloud, "That was the girl in the portrait!" His first impulse was to turn back and return to the doctor's office. But he had had such a negative reaction to her, he did not know if he was ready to apologize. He continued on his way back to the Medallion office.

Samuel Cutter needed a bandage on his knee and a lecture about trying to walk atop a wooden fence, especially one of doubtful strength. Mrs. Cutter marched the eight-year-old out of the office, past Kate and outdoors.

"She would have been happier if I had taken him over my knee and given him a thrashing," Ted muttered to himself. "No doubt that's what that boy needs. Ah, Kate! I didn't see you there."

"Hello, Cousin Ted," she snapped.

"Don't tell me you're in a bad mood, too, lovely one," Ted said, kissing her on the cheek. "I declare, you seem to be in quite a temper, Kate Phenwick."

"I just had an unhappy encounter with a clumsy oaf who nearly knocked me flat on my backside," Kate explained. "My bonnet was knocked askew and my parasol went flying. A brand-new parasol at that!"

"As pretty as you look, I would never guess you had just gone through such a horrifying experience," Ted remarked, amused at her expression. "You weren't injured, were you? I mean, other than your pride."

Kate saw the humor of his statement. "No, I wasn't." She laughed.

"When did all of this occur?"

"As I was coming in your front door, he was going out."

Ted chuckled. "That would have been John Collier. He is a friend of your Cousin Stuart and works for Medallion."

"At that moment, I would have had him fired on the spot!" Kate declared.

"You disliked him that much?"

"I had visions of what might have happened—and my parasol being ruined," Kate replied.

"You are more frivolous than I remembered you to be," Ted remarked. "What else is disturbing you?"

"Edward House, if you must know. It frightens me," Kate explained. "I even asked Marcia if I might sleep with her last night, I was that scared. It's worse than when I was here last autumn."

"The house itself terrifies you?" asked Dr. Ted. "Perhaps you should make arrangements to stay with Jane Augusta while you're here. Her house isn't near as large."

"All winter I lived in dread apprehension of Phenwick House," Kate related. "I was certain it was haunted. I'm still not convinced that it isn't. I largely kept to my room, or went to Mother's suite, completely avoiding the downstairs rooms as often as possible. And I never go to the third floor or down to the basement. My mother says it's me, that I've got some kind of strange notion in my head. I pleaded with her to let me stay in the cottage. Ella could have stayed out there with me, or Patsy O'Plaggerty would have."

"The cottage?"

"The one we call Uncle Michael's cottage," Kate related. "Once spring arrived, I went out to it often. I was so grateful to receive Marcia's letter asking me to come to Boston earlier than planned. Now that I'm here, I find I have a similar fear in Edward House."

"Let me speak to Jane Augusta and see if she won't invite you to stay with her," Ted suggested. "Or perhaps you would rather stay with Peter and Nancy. Those four boys will keep the place lively enough." He took her hand. "But my lovely Kate, I suspect the problem is not in the houses, but in your head. You have an active imagination."

"My imagination?" Kate gasped.

"Fear is usually an inner reaction to some past situation. Then again, it may be something within yourself that is urging you to change your circumstances," Dr. Ted said.

"What do you mean by that?"

"Nature has a way of prodding us in the direction we should be going," Ted related. He winked. "You don't want to be an old maid like Cousin Lydia Ornby, do you? I suspect your fear stems somehow from an innate mating urge, and magnified because your prospects to date appear discouraging."

"Of course I don't want to be an old maid," Kate replied. "Poor Lydia."

"Then I suggest we take steps in the right direction to avoid such a situation," Dr. Ted said.

"But I'm a lady. I haven't met the proper man," Kate stated.

Dr. Ted stroked his beard. "There's a very good chance that you have met him, Kate Phenwick. If I were you, I'd consider taking a second glance at that young man you encountered coming into my office."

Kate gasped as if her cousin had just made the most absurd statement she had ever heard.

# CHAPTER TWENTY-ONE

"Marcia has invited us *both* to supper, John," Stuart called as he was dressing for the occasion. "I accepted for you. Besides, don't you want to meet Rebecca and Kate?"

"I've met them," John returned, reluctantly preparing himself for the evening ahead. "I confess I found more in common with Rebecca than I did with her daughter."

"It is unusual, but not so strange for a younger man to be attracted to an older woman," Stuart remarked as he put the finishing touches to his appearance. "Dr. Ted told me of your collision meeting with Kate. It got you off to a good start."

"I fear it was disastrous," John moaned.

Stuart stood at the door to the other's room. "I passed a flower vendor as I was coming home. I purchased a peace offering for you and a bouquet for my lady love. Admittedly the peonies are more showy, but Marcia is fond of them. The only other flowers the lady had left were violets."

"I can't take violets. They'll make me sneeze."

"I'll carry them for you and give them to Marcia to take to Kate. You will probably never see them again," Stuart commented.

"I feel very uneasy about going to Edward House tonight," John stated. "Fearful, yet with a sense of impending anticipation."

Moments after the young men arrived at the large house on Beacon Hill, Marcia came gliding down the stairs in a lovely white dress, with a skirt so full it covered the width of the stairway. She wore pearls. The white on white was stunning.

"Peonies! My favorite," exclaimed Marcia as she accepted the bouquet and leaned forward to give Stuart a significant kiss. "I'll have them put in my room." She kissed him again.

"And violets for Kate," Stuart said, "from John."

Marcia's eyes twinkled with happiness. "Why are you carrying them, Stuart?"

"Because they make me sneeze," John inserted.

"They were the last flowers the vendor had," Stuart added. "There wasn't any choice. But don't tell Kate."

John sneezed. "Excuse me."

"You carry the peonies, Stuart," Marcia suggested, "and I'll take the violets. You know where the parlor is, John. Why don't you go in there and make yourself comfortable?"

As John watched the loving young couple go up the stairs, his impulse was to leave that house immediately. Maybe he should go away from Boston and the Phenwicks. He questioned his motives. Yet he realized if he did not stay, there would always be an enormous question in his mind.

John went through the library to get to the parlor, stopping a moment at the portrait of Danny, with the image still vividly impressed in his mind, he entered the other room and stood by the likeness of Kate. He could see no identical characteristics between the two. Why should there be? People change with generations.

The door whispered open. Kate was lovely in a soft blue gown, a semi-full skirt. The bodice was low-cut and she wore a cameo on her white skin. She carried a white fan, tied by a ribbon to her wrist. As John turned to see her, he thought the artist had not done justice to that elegant beauty, the fragile features, the sparkling eyes.

"Miss Cathcart?" he questioned as if offering an apology.

"Mr. Collier," returned Kate as she moved into the room. "We meet under more favorable circumstances this time."

"Forgive me for my rude behavior," John said, going to her and taking her hand.

"You were forgiven the instant I received the violets," Kate returned, her smile becoming more radiant as she spoke. "It had been a warm afternoon, and circumstances were not favorable for either of us." She stared into his eyes. "Yes."

"Yes?"

"Yes, Cousin Ted was correct," she stated. "I didn't get a good look at you in all my fury. I was convinced that I had encountered some kind of ogre. I see I was mistaken and I beg that you accept my apology."

"I readily accept, Miss Cathcart."

"You may call me Miss Kate, if you like ... John."

Words were unnecessary as an aura of reality went out from each and mingled with the glow of excitement radiating from the other. John was delighted he had not run away a short while before. Kate was now ecstatic

227

that Marcia had persuaded her to accept the violets and go down to meet John Collier with a positive attitude. After all, accidents did happen.

"Would you care for a stroll about the garden, John?" she asked, feeling slightly uneasy under the increasing penetration of his stare. "Supper will not be for an hour or more. Grandmother will be coming down to join us in the dining room. I've never known her to do that."

"I would enjoy a stroll with you in the garden, Miss Kate," John assured her.

"The wisteria is in bloom," Kate said. "The arbor is dripping with blossoms. I heard peepers for the first time in the pond last night. I love the sounds of nature—especially at Greenfield." She reached to take his hand. "Come along."

Patricia had prepared herself through the afternoon. She had to rest between efforts, causing those who were assisting her to become slightly edgy. Now that she was ready, she sent everyone away and sat in her thronelike chair to relax. She resented being old, the aches and the pains.

Laughter coming from the garden below distracted the old lady. With effort she pushed herself up and found her way to the window. The glare of the sun caused her eyes to water, her vision to blur. At first she saw two young men walking in the garden. They were wearing satin knee breeches and brocaded coats and vests, the style men wore when she was a young girl. She thought of her beloved Edward and how handsome he had appeared to her. Fashions had changed before her courtship with Elias, and he always preferred to wear black.

What were two young men doing dressed like that in her garden? When she thought of Edward, she thought of his stepbrother Danny—and peculiarly of their friend, Michael O'Plaggerty. Was it her imagination? It had to be. This was 1855. Men dressed entirely differently now.

A sunbeam reflected in her eyes, creating a glare. She put her hand to shield her eyes from the brightness. When she again focused on the two people below, she was somewhat startled to see they were not two men at all, but Kate and John Collier. She watched for nearly five minutes as laughter began to bubble within her.

Rebecca silently entered the room. "Mother? Are you all right?"

"Oh, Rebecca," Patricia said as she turned about. "I was hoping someone would interrupt me. I was almost becoming giddy with amusement."

"What is it, Mother?"

"A combination of memories, intrigue and romance," Patricia recited. "My dear Rebecca, will you kindly run an errand for me? There is a large folio in the library near the portrait of Danny—on the bottom shelf. You can't miss it, it's quite large. Clayton Latshaw's name is on it. Will you bring it to me? While you're at it, will you send one of the servants out to ask Kate and Mr. Collier to come to my room?"

"I don't quite understand, Mother. What are you about?"

"It is not important that you know at the present," Patricia returned. "After you bring me the folio, I wish for you to tell the cook that supper may be delayed another fifteen minutes."

Rebecca gazed strangely at her mother, but went to do her bidding as Patricia returned to the window.

# CHAPTER TWENTY-TWO

"I feel as if I have known you forever, Miss Kate," John confessed as they stood beneath the wisteria arbor.

"It's funny how you seemed a stranger just the other day," Kate stated. "Today we're like old friends in such a short matter of time." It was another feeling than she had had with either Ronald Boggs or Paul Ornby. Something definitely was tugging her toward this man and she felt he was resisting coming toward her only out of propriety.

How close they had come to a kiss before they were interrupted by the servant announcing Patricia's wishes. Hand in hand they walked silently toward the house. Kate wondered if it were all happening too suddenly, if she were being irrational in her feelings. John wanted to speculate on so many different things. He desired her to be the person for whom he had been searching; yet were his desires not so intense that he, too, was being irrational?

Patricia was back in her favorite chair when the young couple arrived at her sitting room. She welcomed Kate with a kiss. "You, too, John Collier, come and give me a kiss on the cheek. It's high time we were becoming better acquainted."

John kissed her patronizingly, then he sat beside Kate on the love seat where Patricia indicated that they should. The old lady could tell by their expressions that they found great happiness in one another.

"I see a magical beauty in your faces, Kate and John," Patricia stated. "I hope what I see matures in the fullness of time to a radiant star, two radiances come together to create the brightest star in all the heavens. I must explain that I have always been a poetess—no doubt you've read some of my poetry—if you haven't, you should have."

"I've read your poems, Grandmother," Kate assured her.

"Then you must read them to John sometime," Patricia returned as she rolled a large ring about her finger. "They may well be forgotten in time and of no importance, but I like to feel I made some sort of mark on the world. That is neither here nor there. It is my way of apologizing for being a romantic—no, not apologizing, simply explaining. Rest assured, I have known what love is."

"Love?"

"Yes, love," Patricia affirmed. "I know how some people are almost automatically magnetized together as if they always belonged. They cannot help themselves or resist. Love has forever been there for them, it was theirs but to discover. Oh, what a magnetic pull that can be! Then there are others who simply meet through a physical attraction, through an innate mating urge and the instinct for reproduction. I do not mean to discount that in the least. I have succumbed to several urges and instincts in my life. Don't be shocked. I believe in being candid. But love! Ah, that was the beautiful part of my life, the magic, the glorious! It includes physical expression, but there's something more, something far greater than any other kind of human relationship. The physical thing passes with time, but the inner love continues—perhaps beyond the spheres. Certain people in this day and age would be shocked to hear me express this in such a way. But I've always delighted in shocking people. I hope you are not offended by my words."

"Not at all," John replied. "I think they're beautiful."

"So do I, Grandmother," Kate replied. She rose and went to kiss the lady on the cheek. When she returned to where John was seated, their eyes met in unspoken expressions.

"John, will you be so kind as to unfasten this folio for me?" Patricia asked, indicating the one Rebecca had brought from the library. "Do either of you know the name Clayton Latshaw?"

"He was a preacher," Kate said automatically.

"He was a teacher," John stated almost simultaneously as he rose to go to the folio, which was on a table.

"You are both correct," Patricia stated. "But isn't it curious you should have mentioned those occupations?"

Kate said, "Of course, he is the portrait painter. I wonder why I said preacher?"

"I wonder, too," Patricia returned. "Certain things come to mind for a reason. I want you both to look at the sketches included in Clayton's folio. They were drawn many, many years ago. It is a special collection I have kept and shown only to a few choice friends."

Kate was beside John as he opened the case. "Why, they're sketches of young boys."

233

"All of them?"

"All of them," Patricia replied. "Boys at games and at meditation; boys clothed and boys naked; romping adolescents during a carefree youth that has long since gone by. Still I wonder."

"Edward," Kate said as she stared at a picture.

"Let me see, hold it up," Patricia ordered. "Yes."

"Danny," John said, holding up a second likeness. "I can tell from the expression on the painting in the library."

"Perhaps that is why," Patricia commented, punctuating with a slight cough as her amusement increased.

"Mickey," Kate stated, looking at a third sketch.

"Mickey?" questioned Patricia.

John looked into Kate's face. He whispered, "Mickey?"

"Oh yes, I recall. Edward once told me that his friend was nicknamed Mickey. He was of Irish descent, you know."

"It's really Michael O'Plaggerty, isn't it, Grandmother?" Kate asked.

"They're of the same three boys over and over again," John remarked, after taking his intense gaze from Kate's face. "They're very well drawn and good likenesses."

"How would you know that?" Patricia asked.

"I'm no connoisseur," John explained, "but I can tell if something is well drawn."

"That is not what I meant," the old lady said, attempting to contain the thrill of excitement that was going through her. "How did you know about the likenesses?"

"I suppose it was a guess."

"Was it . . . *really*?" Patricia smiled broadly.

Both John and Kate instinctively knew what she was driving at. They both blushed.

"Why have you shown us these, Grandmother?" Kate

asked, after reviewing the sketches several times. "Mother has often said that the notorious Patricia Phenwick does not do something unless there is a reason behind it."

John tied the folio and returned to the love seat where Kate had gone.

"I have been keeping these for a longer space of time than I care to admit," Patricia explained. "Edward asked me to watch over them. Perhaps my vigilance has not been acute, but I've been aware of where they were kept. Now as the sands of time seem to be slipping from me, I felt I should specially bequeath them into other hands. I want you to have them, Kate. I believe they will mean something to you."

"I would love to have them," Kate replied. "But why would you think they would be something special to me?"

"Only a premonition," Patricia sighed. "Now, seeing your reaction to them—both of your reactions to them—I am convinced my intuition is correct. You will take the folio with you when you return to Greenfield after the wedding."

"Are you sending me home so soon, Grandmother?"

"Yes," Patricia said bluntly, "but I'm going to keep your mother here."

"Return to eerie old Phenwick House alone?" Kate asked, a tremble of fear shuddering through her at the thought.

"Not alone." Patricia smiled. "Ella Shane is there. She'll be your chaperone."

"Chaperone?" Kate questioned.

"It's only proper—if John Collier goes with you."

"Me?"

"Wouldn't you like to see Greenfield?" Patricia inquired. "According to Ted you seem to have quite an interest in the place."

"You've spoken with Dr. Ted?"

"Just this afternoon," Patricia affirmed. "We had quite a long discussion. He—as I do—believes you are two moral young people who seem to have some sort of destiny together. I won't speculate too far into the future—I'm not a seer—but I expect you will learn many things about each other—and about Greenfield—by making such a visit. Besides, I want to spend a longer time with Rebecca, without the interference of her daughter. Not that I don't love you, Kate, and enjoy your being here—I do. But I do want time alone with Rebecca after all these years."

"But will she—?"

"Don't ask further questions," Patricia said with a sigh. "The two of you go find Marcia and Stuart. I'm about to make an entrance, and I don't care to make the effort without an audience."

# CHAPTER TWENTY-THREE

Susannah arrived on the newest ship in the Medallion fleet, the *Patricia*. Accompanying her were her husband, Jim Cornhill, Marcia's brother, Gregory, and Joanna Phenwick. The ship docked a week before the wedding. Arrangements were made for Susannah and Jim to stay with Patricia, Joanna with Nancy and Peter, and Gregory with Stuart. Every night before the wedding was a series of banquets given by members of the Phenwick and Ornby families. Even Jane Augusta opened her house to the horde of relatives. Happiness prevailed. It would be one of the largest weddings Boston had known, the most expensive, the most elaborate and the most extravagant. Marcia and Stuart were wonderfully in love and their joy was shared by all.

Gregory was pleased that his sister was marrying Stuart. Although they lived an ocean apart, Gregory had always kept up correspondence with his friend. Joshua was in charge of Medallion in London, but Gregory was second in authority. He had developed into a handsome young man.

In all the excitement over the wedding, the relationship between Kate and John Collier increased. Each day they found more and more they liked about the other, things that they had in common. There was no playing coy or elusive in any way. They simply knew each other and accepted the fact that they were to fall in love—which they did with no effort at all.

Rebecca observed the relationship growing from friendship into love as she recalled her days of courtship with Johnny Ornby. At first she had rejected Patricia's suggestion that she remain in Boston while Kate and John went together to Greenfield.

"Don't you trust your daughter?" Patricia asked.

"Of course I do."

"And don't you trust John Collier?"

"Mother, he is a man."

"A blessing for which we must be thankful, Rebecca. Have faith in the young people. Love will bloom and mature when it is time, and none of our interference will stop it. But I have great faith in Kate and John. And if things go as I believe they will, we're liable to have another wedding in late summer or early autumn. That would be nice. I would like to see both my granddaughters married before—"

"Before? What are you thinking, Mother?"

"Of the inevitable. Please stay with me for a while, Rebecca. After Susannah and the rest have returned to England, I want us to have time together."

"To make up for the years of being separated?" Rebecca asked, trying not to sound bitter.

"Perhaps a closeness will come at last."

"Mother, do you actually believe that Great-grandfather and Uncle Mike—?"

"That is something we will never really know, Rebecca," Patricia stated. "But in my romantic—perhaps fictional—way of looking at things, wouldn't it be nice if two lonely souls finally found happiness together?"

"I don't understand. I just don't understand."

The wedding was gorgeous, the gowns artistic creations, the principals glowing with beauty. Since the actual ceremony was performed in the late morning, the reception and partying continued through the afternoon and evening. Edward House was radiant and alive with people.

When their expected duties were completed, Kate and John managed to get away by themselves. The occasion had sparked a desire in each of them. While they shared the happiness of Marcia and Stuart, their own inner contentment with each other was magnifying.

"Are you looking forward to returning to Greenfield, dearest Kate?" John asked as they strolled away from the festivities.

"I still have fear and apprehension about the old house."

"Do you actually believe it is haunted?"

"I hear strange noises when I'm in it," Kate confessed. "And I get an eerie feeling when I look at the portraits. Ever since I heard that Margaret went mad in the house, I have imagined I've heard her wailings. And twice I would have sworn I saw an apparition resembling the portrait of Augusta Phenwick stalking through the halls, then just sort of drifting out of sight. There were times I felt as if she were trying to tell me something. And the scent of violets."

"I'm not looking forward to encountering that," John said, "the way I sneeze whenever I'm near them."

"Maybe we shouldn't go to Greenfield after all."

"I think we must, Kate. I have been compelled toward it for a long time—perhaps for all my life. It's as if I feel certain answers will come through by our going there."

"Then we must go, my darling," Kate whispered. "But the day after tomorrow seems so soon."

"Ah, there you are," Dr. Ted exclaimed as the young couple returned to where the guests were still mingling. "I can see you've forgiven this young scamp for knocking your parasol away on the day of your meeting."

"That has been the only time we've ever had a negative feeling toward one another," John stated. "Maybe at that time we were really annoyed at ourselves, but took it out on the other."

"That's an interesting thought," the doctor remarked. "I spoke to my son Joseph about that little experiment we discussed. He will be willing to help us. However, with you going away in the next day or so, I'm certain it can wait until you come back."

"Experiment?" Kate questioned.

"Dr. Ted was going to see if he could hypnotize me," John related. "Someday it might be interesting to see what turns up from such an experiment, but I wonder if it's necessary."

"Not necessary." Ted chuckled and stroked his beard. "I understand you're taking Clayton Latshaw's sketches back to Greenfield with you. Aunt Patricia is delighted about that."

"What significance do they have, Dr. Ted?" Kate questioned.

"To me, none whatsoever," the doctor replied. "But it's what they mean to you that's important, Kate. They may be part of the missing link to that puzzle we've all been working on. I don't usually drink excessively, but this is a real occasion. Oh, when you return from Greenfield, I would like to have a chat with both of you concerning your reactions to Phenwick House."

"Our reactions?"

"A little clinical curiosity on my part," Dr. Ted stated. "I was discussing the matter with Joseph. He's interested, too. Incidentally, I definitely am going to London for that series of lectures. Fact is, I'll go back on the *Patricia* when she sails with Susannah, Jim, Joanna and Gregory."

Marcia could not have been happier. There was no doubt in the family that by marrying Stuart she was now the reigning Phenwick woman. A silent nod of approval went to her from Patricia, Susannah, Rebecca and Joanna. She was now the queen of Edward House.

# CHAPTER TWENTY-FOUR

The carriage ride from Portland was the only part of the journey to Greenfield that appeared familiar to John Collier. The way along the road was heavily forested on the left, but occasionally the river and ultimately the bay could be seen for stretches on the right. It was up hill and down over the irregular terrain. Then came Mill Road and the large forest between it and the village.

"In through there," John said as he pointed to the forest, "is the old Indian camp, isn't it?"

Kate smiled and nodded her head.

John was absorbed in watching the scenery. Now he was almost certain why it all appeared so familiar to him. That is, if he could believe in the theory expressed by Dr. Ted and his son Joseph, who was far more knowledgeable about the subject than his father.

The carriage turned on Old Main Street, going past the Phenwick orchard and the turnoff to the old house itself.

"The carriage will take us to the square in the village," Kate informed him when he wondered why they had not gone directly to the house.

Soon they went by the line of cottages along the lane which belonged to the Phenwicks, the old section of town and into the center of it. They stopped in front of the hotel across from the schoolhouse.

"What do we do from here?" asked John.

"Do you feel like walking?" Kate returned. "We can leave the luggage at the hotel and send Osgood Wymer to pick it up later on."

"I'll trust everything to the hotel except Clayton Latshaw's sketches," John said, taking her hand as they went into the hotel to make arrangements about the bags.

Soon they were walking back through the old town, where most of the buildings had been converted into living quarters for some of the poorer mill workers. There was only one small store and a boardinghouse (which used to be the only hotel) left in business. The scenery did not look familiar to John until they turned down Cottage Lane and he got a first glimpse of the rear view of Phenwick House.

"We could cut through the pasture and go by the garden," Kate suggested.

"The sea cottage is down this lane, isn't it?" John asked. "I'd like to go have a look at it."

"Are you certain you haven't been to Greenfield?"

"Not in this life." He laughed and squeezed her hand.

John stopped in front of the house in which Osgood Wymer lived. He stared at it for some time.

"While we're here, I might as well tell Osgood to go fetch the luggage from the hotel. It will only take a minute," Kate said.

John continued just gazing at the house until Kate returned. She reached for his hand, which was resting on the fence.

"What are you thinking?"

"How dimly familiar everything is," John stated. "It almost brings tears to my eyes. I love you, Kate."

"I think that's the hundredth time you've said that today," Kate returned.

"Only the hundredth. It seems a century since I told anyone that," John said. "Maybe it was—or longer."

"I'm certain, beyond all doubt, that I love you, John."

He wanted to kiss her. She wanted to kiss him. But the open road was hardly the place for it.

As they reached the stable, John stopped. "The stable."

"A clever observation," Kate teased.

"The old one burned down," he commented. "It was a terrible fire."

"Do you actually remember all of this?"

"No. But when I come near to various places, pictures suddenly flash into my mind," John said. "Maybe like Cousin Joseph Ornby suggested, I am really clairvoyant or something like that and these things that flash into my mind are only vibrations from the past that I'm somehow able to pick up."

They kissed behind the stable. In his excitement, John nearly dropped the folio of Clayton Latshaw's drawings. They were interrupted as Osgood Wymer headed toward the stable. They pretended only to have stopped for a minute.

Tremors of anticipation were leaping through John as they went through the gate to the sea cottage.

"One of the first things I'm going to do," John remarked, "is run down to the ocean and sit on a big rock, stare out and think of my mother. I promised I would do that one day. Every time I'm near the ocean, I look at it and think of her. I almost know she picks up my thoughts. But this place is very special, because I know the ocean—even without seeing it—and the beach around it in front of the cottage and down the cliff is the one I dreamed of so often and wrote about in my book. I wonder how I know that."

They slipped through the old gate which needed mending and went to the side of the cottage. John was about to kiss her again when a voice called from within.

"Is that you, Kate Phenwick? What are you doing out there?" Ella Shane appeared at the window. "Fact is, what are you doing back in Greenfield? And who's that with you?"

"Ella, this is John Collier," Kate introduced. "Ella is my governess."

"And who is John Collier?" Ella asked suspiciously.

"He's my lover," Kate answered proudly.

"Kate Phenwick!" Ella exclaimed. "The very idea!"

"Kate is having a game with you, Ella," John corrected. "I love her and she loves me, but we're not—well, we're not married yet so we're not—"

"You'd better *not*," Ella warned, shaking a finger. "Where's your mother, Kate Phenwick?"

"In Boston."

"My word! She allowed you to return to Greenfield—alone—with this—man?" Ella sputtered.

"May we come in and look around at the cottage, Ella? John will be staying out here for a while."

"You didn't answer my question," Ella called as the couple moved around the cottage to the front door.

Kate explained the situation to Ella as best she could. Ella was still not convinced that everything was on the up and up. John investigated about the cottage. He was standing before the portrait of Rebecca when Kate joined him.

"That's Mother when she was a young lady," Kate explained.

"Yes. I know."

Ella stationed herself in the cottage to scrutinize the actions of the couple. She had once been in love herself and she recognized all the symptoms. After she was over the initial shock, the older woman was happy for the young people, became less suspicious and permitted them to go to the big old house by themselves.

"The chapel," John exclaimed as they got near the cemetery on their left, across the lane from Phenwick House.

"I understand it was once used to hold religious services," Kate said. "Now it's only used for funerals. There are crypts beneath it. I have a fear of entering it."

"Do you mind if I examine the headstones in the yard?" John asked, leading her by the hand as they entered. He went almost directly to the section wherein the O'Plaggertys were laid to rest. Timothy. Molly Righteous. "Rit," he said as he ran his fingers over the carved name of Righteous O'Plaggerty.

Beside Righteous was the grave of Michael O'Plaggerty.

"The stones have been neglected," John commented. "I'll have to straighten them. Shall we go into the house?"

They entered through the breezeway, going into the back part of the house first. The servants were all in their quarters. Nobody was about. The floors groaned beneath their weight.

"Let's go into the study first," John suggested.

"Oh, I hate that room. It has always terrified me. Even when Papa was alive it was a horror to me," Kate said.

"For just a minute."

They entered the room. Kate was prepared to react as

she always had. She did not. Instead a great sense of peace came over her. Even the portrait of Danny suddenly looked beautiful to her.

"I can't believe it," she murmured. "I've never felt so serene in this room."

"Let's go across to the sitting room," John suggested as he looked from the likeness in the portrait to Kate's face. John had a satisfied feeling as he made the observation.

"So that is the original of Augusta Phenwick," John stated as they entered the sitting room. "What a grand and powerful lady she must have been."

Kate stood in awe. "I don't know how many times I've stared at that portrait until I felt intimidated by it. For the first time it seems as if she is smiling."

The room suddenly became drenched with the scent of violets. John took Kate in his arms and kissed her. The odor intensified.

"Well, Augusta, you're not such a bad old girl after all," John exclaimed before he kissed Kate again.

Was there the sound of distant laughter and a whispered: "*Happiness*"?

"The violets! Do you smell them, John?"

He breathed deeply. "Yes, I smell them. And they *don't* make me sneeze!" He looked up at the portrait and winked. "You're a sly old girl, Augusta!"

"The house has become friendly to me, John," Kate observed after another kiss. "That sinister quality has gone. I don't know how it happened, but it's wonderful."

Another kiss.

"My darling, now I want to walk down on the beach," John said.

A refreshing breeze rose from the ocean. The calm

and restful movement of the tide, the lapping waves seemed to be singing to the young couple as they walked over the sandy beach, climbed about the rocks.

"I doubt if either of us will understand what truly has happened," John said as they sat on a rock together and he had concentrated for nearly five minutes on thoughts of his mother.

"I don't think it really matters *what* has happened," Kate said, "as long as it has happened."

"Whether it's true or not, I do believe you are my soul mate, Kate. I don't believe either of us will be content *anywhere* without the other."

"I'm not thoroughly convinced about the idea of soul mates," Kate said after a few moments' pause. "It's a lovely notion. I doubt if my curiosity will ever be completely resolved."

"My curious Kate."

"But I want to believe in a kind of magic that has brought our love into reality, John."

They rose from the rock upon which they had been sitting. John took her in his arms and kissed her as if he were dedicating his life to her.

"I love you so very much, Kate."

"Of one thing I'm certain, I am and will always be the happiest Phenwick woman of all."

As they kissed again, she instinctively knew that the sense of mystery that had haunted her up until then had been lifted.

## CAST OF CHARACTERS

| | |
|---|---|
| JOHN COLLIER | A handsome young man from Illinois, who has been haunted by disturbing dreams. |
| NELLIE | His sister. |
| TOM | His brother. |
| WILMA | His mother. |
| HOMER DILLSWORTH | A traveling tonic salesman and con artist. |
| CLARENCE HOSKINS | A self-styled private detective. |
| ELLA SHANE | Kate's governess and Rebecca's longtime friend. |
| OSGOOD WYMER | Handyman at Phenwick House. |
| CORA BEATON | Housekeeper at Phenwick House. |
| CASPAR RIDDLE | Butler at Phenwick House. |
| RONALD BOGGS | A local Greenfield boy who has grown up with Kate. |
| PATSY O'PLAGGERTY | Kate's best friend. |
| FANNY MOCKERTY | Kate's second best friend. |
| ALICE MUMFORD | Daughter of an old Greenfield family. |
| EDWARD PAUL ORNBY | Kate's distant cousin. |
| CARMEN | A New Orleans fortune-teller. |
| BILL SIMMONS | A bartender at the Seagull Tavern in Savannah. |
| DELBERT LONGNECK | A seasoned sailor. |

# THE PHENWICKS

| | |
|---|---|
| **AUGUSTA** | Founder of the family. She maintains an eerie hold over the surviving members. |
| **DANIEL** | Augusta's only son who lived to adulthood. Father of Elias (by Kate Mumford); married to Margaret O'Plaggerty, and father of Alexander, Peter and Rachel. |
| **ELIAS** | Married to Patricia Kelburn; father of Rebecca. |
| **REBECCA** | Only daughter of Elias and Patricia, first married to Johnny Ornby, becoming foster-mother to Adrianne and Lydia; second marriage to Robert Cathcart; mother of Kate Phenwick. |
| **KATE PHENWICK** | Daughter of Rebecca and granddaughter of Patricia. She is a young beauty disturbed by the sensation that the houses of the Phenwick family haunt her with distant memories. |
| **ALEXANDER** | Married to Susannah Phenwick and adopted father of Marcia and Gregory. |
| **MARCIA** | An English peasant girl adopted with her brother into the Phenwick family. |
| **GREGORY** | Handsome brother of Marcia. Resides in England. |
| **PETER** | Married to Helen Barnfather; father of Augustus, Joanna, Prentise and Joshua. Second marriage to Nancy Cox; father of Thadius, John, Paul and Daniel. |
| **NANCY** | Peter's lovely wife. |
| **AUGUSTUS** | Peter's eldest son, married to |

|  | Lillian Webb and father of Stuart and Gordon. |
|---|---|
| STUART | Eldest son of Augustus, now head of Medallion Enterprises in Boston. |
| GORDON | Second son of Augustus, an ordained minister in a fundamentalist church. |
| JOANNA | An actress who has remained unwed. Only daughter of Peter. |
| PRENTISE | Peter's second son, married to Harriet Pettijohn. Head of Medallion in Savannah. |
| JOSHUA | Peter's third son, married to Olivia Pritchard. Joshua is head of Medallion in London. |
| RACHEL | Daniel's only daughter. Died in her teens. |
| EDWARD | Adopted son of Augusta; married to Patricia Kelburn; father of Susannah and David. |
| PATRICIA | The widow of both Edward and Elias, she has long been the matriarch of the Phenwick family. Mother of Susannah and Rebecca, |
| DAVID | Edward's only son, killed in the War of 1812. |
| SUSANNAH | Edward's daughter, married to Alexander and foster-mother of Marcia and Gregory. |
| JANE | Adopted daughter of Augusta; married to Jeffrey Ornby; mother of Frederick, Johnny and Andrew. |
| FREDERICK | Jane's eldest son. |
| JOHNNY | A doctor, father of Adrianne and Lydia by his first wife; second marriage to Rebecca; no children. |

ADRIANNE        Eldest daughter of Johnny.
                Murdered in England.

LYDIA           Second daughter of Johnny. An
                old maid with many emotional
                problems.

ANDREW          Third son of Jane. Married to
                Livinia Hendricks; father of
                Jane Augusta, Daniel, Theo-
                dore, Angela, Bertha and Jef-
                frey.

JANE AUGUSTA    Andrew's eldest daughter; mar-
                ried to Eustace Clark, now wid-
                owed. No children. She is the
                matriarch of the Ornby side of
                the family.

DANIEL          Eldest son of Andrew. An at-
                torney. Married to Melissa Kes-
                ler; father of James, Henry,
                Thomas and Sarah.

THEODORE        Andrew's second son. A physi-
                cian interested in psychology.
                Married to Louise Lacy; father
                of Joseph, Augustus, Collin,
                Mary Rose and Ruth.